Books by Laurien Berenson

A PEDIGREE TO DIE FOR
UNDERDOG
DOG EAT DOG
HAIR OF THE DOG
WATCHDOG
HUSH PUPPY
UNLEASHED
ONCE BITTEN
HOT DOG
BEST IN SHOW
JINGLE BELL BARK
RAINING CATS AND DOGS
CHOW DOWN
HOUNDED TO DEATH
DOGGIE DAY CARE MURDER
GONE WITH THE WOOF
DEATH OF A DOG WHISPERER
THE BARK BEFORE CHRISTMAS
LIVE AND LET GROWL
MURDER AT THE PUPPY FEST
WAGGING THROUGH THE SNOW
RUFF JUSTICE
BITE CLUB
HERE COMES SANTA PAWS
GAME OF DOG BONES
HOWLOWEEN MURDER

Published by Kensington Publishing Corporation

# Here Comes
# Santa Paws

## LAURIEN
## BERENSON

KENSINGTON BOOKS
www.kensingtonbooks.com

KENSINGTON BOOKS are published by
Kensington Publishing Corp.
119 West 40th Street
New York, NY 10018

All Kensington titles, imprints and distributed lines are available at special quantity discounts for bulk purchases for sales promotion, premiums, fund-raising, educational or institutional use. Special book excerpts or customized printings can also be created to fit specific needs. For details, write or phone the office of the Kensington Special Sales Manager: Kensington Publishing Corp., 119 West 40th Street, New York, NY, 10018. Attn. Special Sales Department. Phone: 1-800-221-2647.

Kensington and the K logo Reg. U.S. Pat. & TM Off.

ISBN-13: 978-1-4967-1846-4
ISBN-10: 1-4967-1846-1
First Kensington Hardcover Edition: October 2019
First Kensington Mass Market Edition: October 2020

ISBN-13: 978-1-4967-1847-1 (ebook)
ISBN-10: 1-4967-1847-X (ebook)

10 9 8 7 6 5 4 3 2 1

Printed in the United States of America

# Here Comes
# Santa Paws

"I suppose they could have done worse," Aunt Peg grumbled.

*You think?*

Margaret Turnbull was an acknowledged authority on all things canine. A longtime Standard Poodle breeder and an experienced dog show judge, she adored dogs of all shapes and sizes. She understood their moods and their personalities. She could shape their characters and predict their actions. And every dog Aunt Peg had ever met adored her right back.

Those three puppies had no idea how lucky they were.

"What breed are they?" I asked.

I knew she'd have an answer ready. A normal person might have labeled the puppies cuddly or cute. Not Aunt Peg. I was sure she'd already been busy assessing the tiny canines' features and cataloging their good qualities. It was no surprise that she came up with a quick reply.

"Australian Shepherds, unless I miss my guess. Two blacks and a blue merle. Maybe not entirely purebred, but close enough to have the look. They seem healthy enough, even after having spent part of the night outside. But I still don't understand what they're doing here. Why would someone have left them at the end of my driveway?"

"Probably because your reputation precedes you," I said. "Maybe someone had an accidental litter and was too lazy to do right by them. They figured you'd give the puppies a good home."

"Find them one is more like it," she replied. "I'll fatten them up, worm them, get them their shots, then locate some lovely people for them in January. They're young and appealing. That will help."

"I love puppies," I said dreamily. It had been years

# Chapter One

"Guess what I found in my Christmas stocking this morning?" Aunt Peg said.

I paused, holding the phone to my ear. Where Aunt Peg was concerned, a guess was a risky venture. Seventy years old and sharp as a bee sting, she made it her mission to keep me on my toes.

Her interests were wide ranging, encompassing everything from her beloved Standard Poodles, to global politics, to the psychology behind reality TV. But most of all, she enjoyed stirring up trouble.

And since I was the one who was usually left holding the bag when her escapades backfired, you can probably understand why I stopped and thought before I answered. And then attempted to dodge the question entirely.

"Christmas is still two and a half weeks away," I replied. "Why would anyone be leaving presents in your stocking now?"

"That's what I'd like to know," she huffed. "And this most certainly wasn't a present. At least not a welcome one."

"Oh?"

"Oh?" she mimicked. "Is that all you have to say?"

"I'm waiting for more information."

"So am I."

I sighed under my breath. As usual, I didn't have time to waste. I'm a wife, a mother to two growing boys, and a special needs tutor at a private school. I also have five Standard Poodles of my own, plus a small spotted mutt, who thinks he's another Poodle.

*And* Christmas was coming.

So I needed to move this conversation along. "I'm a little busy here," I said. "Give me a hint. Animal, mineral, or vegetable?"

"Animal."

Hmm.

I'd fully expected her to say *mineral*. If Santa had left a lump of coal in Aunt Peg's stocking, I wouldn't have been surprised. She and I both would have had a good laugh about that.

Well, I would have anyway. But no such luck.

"Puppies!" Aunt Peg announced. She'd obviously grown tired of waiting for me to come up with an answer on my own. "Some depraved person tucked a litter of three into my Christmas stocking. The poor things look like they're no more than five weeks old."

"What?" I yelped.

Faith, the big black Poodle who was lying draped across my lap, lifted her head and tipped it to one side. My shriek had probably hurt her ears. Faith and I have been together for nearly nine years. She knew what I was thinking almost before I did. Now she had to be wondering what was the matter. I patted her reassuringly.

When she settled back down, I returned to the conversation. "You can't be serious. Are you saying that somebody snuck into your house last night with an armful of puppies?"

The thought defied belief, but I still had to ask.

"Good Lord, Melanie, do try to keep up. Of course nobody came inside the house. Otherwise the dogs would have raised the alarm, and I would have confronted the intruder with a shotgun."

Aunt Peg doesn't actually have a shotgun. Just so you know. She does, however, stand six feet tall and have a grip that can make a grown man wince. Even her glare is fearsome. Given a choice, most people would probably rather face down the weapon.

"I'm talking about the stocking that's hanging from the mailbox post at the end of my driveway," she said. "I put it up last week and it looks quite festive, if I do say so myself. It's *supposed* to be a holiday decoration. Nobody was meant to put it to use."

"Christmas puppies," I said with a slow, happy, smile. "Cool."

"Cut that out," Aunt Peg snapped. "This isn't a holiday fairy tale. Those puppies were abandoned. They're homeless."

"Not anymore," I pointed out. I was glad she couldn't see that I was still smiling. Even Faith looked happy now. Talking about puppies has that effect on both of us. "Now they have you."

since I'd had a litter of my own. "Can I come and see them?"

"I thought you were busy." Aunt Peg's tone was arch.

"That was before you told me you had puppies. See you soon!"

I disconnected before she had time to argue. I was sliding Faith off my lap when my husband, Sam, walked around the corner into the living room. Tall and fit, he carried himself with an easy grace. When he smiled—which he did often—his gray eyes crinkled at the corners. Right now, however, Sam was looking uncharacteristically disgruntled.

His blond hair was mussed, as though he'd been raking his fingers through it, and his denim shirt was partially untucked. I knew Sam had been working in his home office. It didn't look as though things had been going well. No doubt he'd been eager for a distraction.

"Was that Peg?" he asked. "Did I hear you say that she has puppies?"

"Yes, and yes," I replied. "I'm going to go play with them. Want to come along?"

"I wish." He sounded envious. "But *some* of us aren't already on Christmas break."

That was meant to be a jab at my employer, Howard Academy, and their famously liberal policy toward school vacations. The purpose of the extended recess was to allow students' families ample time for their trips to the beach or ski slopes. Fortunately, it also gave teachers and administrators the same three weeks off. None of us complained about that.

I hopped up from the couch, braced my hands on Sam's shoulders, and planted a quick kiss on his lips. "You work for yourself. Doesn't that mean that you get to set your own hours?"

"Sure," he said. "But it also means that if I don't sit down and actually do the work, no one else will either."

The rest of our canine crew must have been keeping Sam company in his office. Now they came trailing into the room behind him. Poodles come in many colors, but all of ours are black—not surprising since most of them are interrelated. All our Standard Poodles were also former show dogs. Each had titles and a long, impressive name that nobody ever bothered to use now that they were retired from the show ring.

Leading the way were the two males, Tar and Augie. Tar wasn't the brightest Poodle we owned, but with numerous Bests in Show on his résumé, he was the most accomplished. Augie belonged to our older son, Davey, who had handled him to his championship. Both dogs were cocky and bold, and they thought they ruled the house. I was pretty sure that one day the three female Poodles would set them straight about that.

Aside from Faith, we also had Sam's older bitch, Raven, and Faith's daughter, Eve. Those girls were funny and sweet, and smarter than the average child. The bitches were less rambunctious than the boys, but they definitely knew how to get their point across when they needed to.

Completing the pack was our newest addition, Bud. A small black-and-white dog of indeterminate heritage, he had been rescued from the side of the road the previous year and had quickly become every bit as much a member of the family as the Poodles were.

Laces clenched between his teeth, Bud was dragging a shoe behind him. It appeared to be one of Davey's sneakers. There were several dozen dog toys scattered throughout the house, but without fail, the little mutt tended to help himself to something that was supposed to be off-limits.

I rescued the shoe and set it on a nearby table. Bud wagged his stubby tail and gave me his doggy grin. Heights didn't deter him for long. We both knew he was just waiting for me to turn my back so he could recapture his prize.

"So what's the story with the puppies?" Sam asked. "I know Peg wasn't expecting a litter. How did she end up with one?"

"She says they're Christmas orphans. Aussie look-alikes, apparently. Dumped at the end of her driveway and in need of good homes."

He gazed at me askance. "Not here. Don't get any ideas about that. We already have a houseful."

"Does that mean there's no room at the inn?" I lifted a brow.

Sam got the none-too-subtle Christmas reference. He grinned reluctantly. "Not unless one of them is pregnant and riding a donkey. In which case, I may be forced to re-consider."

I walked out to the front hallway and grabbed a coat and scarf from the closet. "I won't be gone long. Try not to work too hard while I'm away."

"You'll pick up Kevin on your way home?"

Four-year-old Kevin was our younger son. Mornings, he attended Graceland Nursery School. Like Davey, who was in his first year of high school, Kev still had another week before his Christmas vacation began. I'd be gone from Aunt Peg's in plenty of time to swing by and get him. Or so I thought.

"Sure," I said. "I can handle that. No problem."

* * *

I've never seen a puppy that wasn't adorable, and the three in Aunt Peg's kitchen were no exception. The two males were black with tan markings. A ruff of white hair formed a wide ring around their shoulders and chests. The lone female was a blue merle with bright blue eyes. All three stared at me inquisitively when I sat down on the floor beside the low, newspaper-lined pen Aunt Peg had erected for them.

She and I lived in neighboring towns in lower Fairfield County, Connecticut, so it hadn't taken me very long to find my way to her kitchen. From my home in North Stamford, it was just a short trip down the Merritt Parkway to her house in back country Greenwich.

At ten o'clock in the morning, the scenic highway had been nearly empty. Though the Stamford mall and trendy Greenwich Avenue were bound to be thronged with holiday shoppers, I'd gone well north of either destination. Christmas carols blasting from my radio, I'd spent the trip singing along. Thankfully, I'd been alone, so no one else had had to suffer through it.

Aunt Peg had met me at the front door, with her pack of Standard Poodles eddying around her legs. The dogs and I were old friends, and I'd greeted each one by name. They'd then formed an honor guard around us as I followed Aunt Peg through the house.

Her kitchen was cozy. It smelled like warm scones. And best of all, there were puppies. It was like the trifecta of all good things.

Except that now Aunt Peg was hovering above me as I sat on her floor. Her hands were propped on her hips, and she was frowning downward at the three Aussie puppies, who were frolicking happily in their pen.

"They're just *babies*," I said, delighted. I reached out and picked up the blue girl. Her hair was silky soft, and when I lifted her to my face, she nuzzled my chin with her nose. I inhaled the delicious scent of puppy breath. "They're not even steady on their feet yet."

"I told you they were young." Aunt Peg sighed. "Those puppies should never have been separated from their dam this early. It's criminal what some people will do."

I glanced up over my shoulder. "You have no idea who left them here?"

"None, even though I've given it plenty of thought. I know every dog in the neighborhood—or at least I thought I did. And I can't think of a single one who could have produced puppies that look like these."

Aunt Peg's neighborhood had formerly been farm country. The barns and meadows were now long gone, however, and the narrow lanes had been widened and paved. Her road held half a dozen single-family homes, each on a generous five acre lot. Roaming dogs were a rarity there. Nevertheless, I was sure Aunt Peg would have been well acquainted with the local canine population.

"Have you given them names yet?"

Aunt Peg growled under her breath. Naming implied ownership, and we both knew it. Still, she had to call them something, didn't she?

She motioned toward the puppy I had snuggled in my arms. "I call her Blue."

"I would never have guessed," I said with a straight face.

"That one's Black." Aunt Peg pointed at the male puppy who was trying to climb out over the low wooden rail.

Now I was biting back a grin. "I foresee a problem with your naming strategy."

"Not at all." Her chin lifted. She indicated the second boy. "His name is Ditto."

"Oh, that's excellent!" I sputtered out a surprised laugh. "Well done."

"Bear in mind those are only temporary names," Aunt Peg said firmly. "The puppies' new owners will naturally want to change them."

"Naturally," I agreed. "When the time comes."

"Let's hope it's sooner rather than later."

"But not until after the holidays," I pointed out.

Aunt Peg nodded in agreement.

I put the blue girl back in the pen and rescued the boy puppy who was still trying to scramble over the side. He jumped into my hands and immediately began to wriggle around, asking to be lowered to the kitchen floor. I was about to oblige him when my cell phone sounded. Currently, I had it set to squawk like an angry bird.

Aunt Peg spun around and stared at my coat. I'd left it slung over a nearby chair. My phone was in the pocket. "What is that unearthly noise?"

"Cell phone." Still holding the puppy with one hand, I beckoned with the other.

"It sounds ridiculous," Aunt Peg sniffed. She reached over and fished through my pockets.

"Yes, but it's loud so I can always hear it," I told her. She handed me the device, and I held it to my ear. "Hello?"

"Melanie!"

The caller was female. That much I knew immediately. But she was whispering, so I didn't recognize her voice right away. There was no mistaking the urgency in her tone, however.

I lifted the phone away and looked at the caller ID. "Claire? Is that you? Why are you whispering?"

"Melanie, you have to come right away. It's horrible. She's dead!"

A sudden chill washed over me. Claire was family. Married to my ex-husband, Bob, she was stepmother to my older son, Davey. She was also a dear friend. Whatever she needed, I would be there for her.

Quickly I lowered the black puppy to the floor, then gripped the phone with both hands. Aunt Peg was staring at me in concern. I shook my head. I still had no idea what was going on.

"Slow down," I said to Claire. "Take a deep breath. Then tell me what's wrong. Who's dead?"

"Lila Moran. She's a new client of mine. I was just dropping off a few things at her house. She wasn't even supposed to be here. But she is. She's lying on the floor and there's blood everywhere."

# Chapter
## Two

"What's the matter?" Aunt Peg hissed.

I ignored her. She leaned down and poked my shoulder. Hard. I quickly angled away so she couldn't grab the phone out of my hands.

"It's Claire," I said. "Something's happened. Give me a minute."

"Oh God." Claire moaned. "Is that Peg? Don't tell her it's me. I can't deal with her right now. Melanie, you have to come and help me. I don't know what to do."

There was no use in pointing out that Aunt Peg already knew whom I was talking to. Claire clearly wasn't thinking straight. I hoped that meant she was wrong about the dead body too.

"Claire," I said slowly. Calmly. "Breathe." I waited a moment while she did so. "Now tell me what happened."

"I just did!" she wailed, her voice still edging toward panic. "Lila is *dead*!"

Out of the corner of my eye, I saw Aunt Peg flinch. She'd heard that.

"Are you sure?" I asked Claire.

"Of course I'm sure. She's lying right here in front of me."

That wasn't what I'd wanted to know. Not at all.

"Where are you now?" I asked.

"I'm standing in her living room."

"You're alone?" I confirmed. "You're sure you're not in any danger?"

"No," she replied firmly. Then her voice quavered. "At least I don't think so. Oh God, what made you ask *that*? Do you think the person who did this to her is still *here*?"

"I don't know," I said. "I don't know anything yet. Listen to me, Claire. I want you to turn around and walk outside. When you get there, lock yourself in your car. As soon as you've done that, hang up with me and dial nine-one-one. Okay? Can you do that?"

"I'm leaving," Claire told me. "I'm getting out right now. And I've already called nine-one-one. I did that right away. The moment I saw her. In case I was wrong and somebody could still help her. But they can't. It's just that I was just hoping . . ."

There was a moment of silence. I was afraid I'd lost her. Then her voice returned, and I exhaled sharply.

"Okay, I'm outside now. I'm walking toward my car."

"That's good," I said. "Wait in your car until help arrives. The dispatcher said they're sending someone, right?"

"Yes . . . yes, she did," Claire stuttered. "She said help would be here in less than ten minutes. But you have to come too. Melanie, you can't leave me here to face this by myself. I need you!"

"I'm on my way," I said. I was already pushing myself to my feet. "I'll be there as soon as I can. Where are you?"

"Oh. Right. I forgot that part." Claire giggled. I hoped she wasn't becoming hysterical. "I'm in New Canaan. On Forest Glen Lane. It's off Weed Street. I'm at the gatehouse for the Mannerly estate. Do you know where that is?"

"No, but I can find it. I'll be there soon. Are you in your car yet?"

"Yes," she said, and I heard a door thunk shut. "I'm locked in."

"Good. Just stay there," I told her. "Don't move."

"Hurry, okay?" Claire's voice was shaking again. *"Please?"*

I shoved my phone in my pocket and grabbed my coat off the back of the chair. Aunt Peg cleared the Poodles out of our way as we hurried toward the front door, then down the outside steps to the driveway. She fired questions at me as we ran.

"Who's dead?" she immediately wanted to know.

"A woman named Lila Moran."

Aunt Peg frowned. "Who's she?"

"Claire said she was a client."

"Claire's arranging an event for her?"

"I don't know," I said. "Maybe."

Claire had her own event planning business. Her specialty was over-the-top children's birthday parties, but she also worked with a number of corporate clients. Earlier in the fall, Claire had come up with a brilliant idea to expand the services her company offered. She'd announced her availability to act as a personal Christmas shopper for busy Fairfield County residents. She'd quickly found her-self with as many customers as she could handle. Perhaps she'd met Lila Moran that way.

"How did the woman die?" Aunt Peg demanded.

"I don't know that either. Claire didn't say."

"Who killed her?"

I stopped and stared. "How would I know that?"

"You were the one on the phone with her," Aunt Peg snapped in frustration. "I thought surely Claire must have told you *something*."

"She told me she needed help," I said simply. "So I'm going to help her."

"I'm coming with you," Aunt Peg decided suddenly as I reached my car.

We'd dashed out of the house together. Aunt Peg hadn't even stopped to grab a jacket. We hadn't had any snow yet this winter, but the morning temperature was barely above freezing. Aunt Peg was dressed in a cotton turtle-neck, jeans, and sneakers. We'd been outside for only thirty seconds, and already she looked cold.

"No, you're not," I told her. I was holding the car key, but my hand stilled above the door handle. This was non-negotiable.

"I can help too," Aunt Peg said firmly.

"You'll freeze," I pointed out.

"No, I won't. Your car has a heater."

So much for the easy excuse.

"Claire doesn't want you there," I said.

Aunt Peg had started to climb into the Volvo. Now she paused. "Did she say that?"

"Yes."

Aunt Peg's eyes narrowed. I knew she was getting ready to argue again.

"Look," I said. "All I know is that something horrible has happened and that Claire stumbled on the scene. She's understandably upset and she needs our support. What she doesn't need is for you to show up and tell everyone what to do. The police are already on their way. The situation is being handled. Just let me go and get her through this, okay?"

"I guess so," Aunt Peg muttered. She stepped away from the car. "If you insist."

"I'll call later and tell you everything," I said as I slid into my seat.

"You'd better," Aunt Peg replied darkly.


I probably violated a few traffic laws between Greenwich and New Canaan. But I got there quickly and that was all that mattered. Nevertheless, it looked as though half the local police force had already beaten me to the scene.

New Canaan was a quiet, affluent, mostly residential town. There were no shopping malls or fast food restaurants. The town boasted more parks than gas stations. Residents valued their privacy and sent their children to the town's excellent public schools.

Crime was unusual in New Canaan. Violent crime was almost unheard of. So I wasn't surprised that whatever had taken place inside the gatehouse at the Mannerly estate had resulted in a sizable police presence.

Forest Glen was a narrow, winding lane, so I'd already slowed my car to well below the speed limit before the estate came into view. A forbidding-looking wall—its stone base topped by black, wrought iron, spikes—was the first indication that I was nearing my destination. The property itself was densely wooded. I drove for another quarter mile, without seeing a single break in the trees, before I finally arrived at a wide double gate. It, too, was made of iron and stood at least eight feet tall.

Both sides of the gate were open, but a police cruiser was parked across the driveway, blocking access. As the Volvo coasted closer to the entrance, I sat up in my seat and attempted to peer down the driveway. It was deeply shadowed by a solid thicket of tree trunks and encroaching underbrush. A canopy of tangled branches arched in the air above it.

About thirty feet inside the property, and barely visible in the gloom, was a small vine-covered building. Presumably, that was the gatehouse where I would find Claire. I turned on my signal and started to pull over. Immediately, a police officer stepped out into the road to wave me past.

I stopped and rolled down my passenger side window. The officer leaned down and looked inside.

"Ma'am, I'm going to need you to move along," he said.

"I'm here for Claire Travis," I told him. "She's the woman who called and reported what had happened. She's waiting for me at the gatehouse."

At least I hoped she was. I couldn't see her car. But nor could I imagine that the authorities would have let her leave so quickly—certainly not before they'd questioned her and begun to try to figure out what was going on.

"Claire Travis," he repeated slowly. "And you are?"

"Melanie Travis." For once, the fact that I still used my first husband's name actually came in handy.

"You're a relative?" he asked.

"We're sisters," I lied. "Claire called me right after she dialed the emergency number. I was in Greenwich, and I came straight here. Whatever's going on in there, Claire needs my support."

He considered for a few seconds, then nodded. He gestured toward the other side of the road. "Park over there out of the way, and I'll walk you in."

I parked the Volvo and got out. The officer watched with approval as I locked it behind me.

"Stick close to me," he said when I'd joined him in the driveway. "And don't touch anything. Your sister's sitting on a bench behind the gatehouse. As soon as the detectives are finished inside, they're going to want to interview her. I'm not sure if they'll let you stay for that part, but you can wait with her until they're ready."

They would let me stay, all right, I thought. Otherwise Claire and I would both be leaving. But I knew better than to voice the sentiment aloud.

The driveway in front of me was long and barely lit by the weak winter sun. By the time we reached the gatehouse, I still hadn't been able to catch even a glimpse of the main house anywhere ahead of us. The bulk of the estate appeared to be entirely shielded from the road by the overgrown forest.

Idly, I wondered if it belonged to a Hollywood icon or some dot-com billionaire. Clearly, the owner possessed a fanatic need for seclusion. I could well imagine he or she wasn't going to appreciate the authorities mounting an investigation on the property. Even here on the outer edge.

The closer we came to the gatehouse, the more dilapidated it appeared. The compact, one-story building had small windows and faded clapboard siding. Its roof sagged in one corner. There was no Christmas wreath on the front door, nor any holiday lights. Nothing brightened the dwelling's drab exterior.

The officer bypassed the front entrance without pausing. He walked me around the gatehouse to the other side.

I saw Claire's car first. Her red Civic was parked in a small cleared area beside the driveway. Then I finally saw Claire. She was seated on an ancient wooden bench placed just outside the building's back door. Her head was lowered; her shoulders slumped. *Forlorn.* That was the first word that came to mind.

The low branches clustered over the spot must have provided shade in the summer. But the limbs were bare now. Slapping and rattling in the light breeze, they looked threatening, almost malevolent, as they hung down over the small clearing.

I was already hurrying toward her when Claire looked up and saw us. Quickly, she jumped to her feet. A look of relief lit up her face.

Claire was statuesque and slender, with long, dark, hair that was now mostly hidden beneath a knitted cap. Her bulky down parka was zipped all the way up to her chin, and she had fuzzy mittens on her hands. Her face was alarmingly pale. The only spot of color was her nose, which was red from the cold.

"Your sister's here, Ms. Travis," the officer said. "She said you called her and told her to come."

Claire's startled gaze found mine. "Sister?" she murmured.

Quickly I closed the gap between us. I gathered her in my arms for a strong hug. "Just go with it," I said under my breath. "I had to talk my way in. So now we're sisters."

Claire stepped back out of my embrace. The smile she aimed at the policeman made his cheeks flush. "Thank you, Officer Jenkins. I feel so much better now."

"Good." He ducked his head. "I'm sure Detective Hronis will be out to speak with you shortly. I'd better get back to my post." He turned and retreated down the driveway.

"Look at you. You're freezing!" I grasped Claire's hands in mine and rubbed briskly back and forth. "How long have you been sitting out here?"

"I don't know. Maybe fifteen minutes?"

"Why?"

She shrugged. "They told me to sit down and not move. Something about messing up evidence. I didn't really think about it. I just did what they said."

That didn't sound at all like the Claire I knew and loved—a woman who ran her own company and was happy to be in charge. I wondered if she was in shock.

"Your car isn't evidence," I said firmly. "Let's go sit inside there. It's got to be warmer, and at least we'll be out of the wind."

I waited until we were sitting in the Civic's bucket seats and Claire had removed her mittens and scrubbed her hands over her face before saying, "Now—before the police come to ask you questions—tell me what happened."

She sucked in a breath. "I don't know where to begin."

"Start at the beginning. Tell me why you came here this morning."

"Lila is . . . she was . . . a client," Claire said slowly. "You know I started the personal shopper thing, right?"

"Of course." I'd been half-tempted to sign up for her services myself.

"I figured that with Christmas coming, it might prove to be a popular sideline to the event planning. But let me tell you, I had *no* idea. I've been swamped."

"That's because you're good at what you do," I said.

Claire was still jittery. She needed to relax. So I started with the easy stuff. "Walk me through how it works."

"Generally, someone hears about my services, they get in touch, and we agree to meet. Mostly, it's guys because . . ." Her lips quirked in a half-smile. "You know."

"They're lazy, and they hate to shop?"

She nodded. "Either that or they're just unimaginative. And some have jobs that take up so much of their lives, they don't have time to think about anything else."

"So you meet up with a client," I prompted.

"That's right. We talk about their Christmas lists and the people they need to buy gifts for. They tell me about their preferences and the kinds of things they like to give, like maybe books or wine. I take some notes about the people I'll be shopping for and make suggestions about things that might work. After that, we discuss how much they want to spend, and then I'm pretty much good to go."

"So you did all those things with Lila Moran?"

"Yes. About three weeks ago. In fact, we met right here at her home."

"So why did you come back this morning? Were the two of you supposed to meet again?"

"No." Claire frowned. "That's what's so strange. Lila wasn't supposed to be here at all. After I've bought a few presents for a client, I usually go ahead and gift wrap everything. Then, if they don't want to be bothered picking stuff up, I can deliver. That was what Lila had asked me to do."

"Tell me what you saw when you arrived."

"Nothing." She stopped and shook her head. "I mean, everything *seemed* normal. I had no reason to think it wouldn't be."

"Had you made a delivery for Lila previously?"

"Yes, last week. I went in the back door, piled the packages on her kitchen table, and left. I thought today would be the same. So I drove back here and parked. I unloaded her things from my trunk and let myself in."

"How did you do that?" I asked. "Do you have a key?"

"No, but Lila keeps one under the flowerpot on the stoop."

Both our gazes swiveled that way. The empty clay pot was now sitting on its side. "Not exactly high-tech security," I said drily.

"Believe me, nothing about this place is high-tech," Claire told me. "Lila grumbled about that a lot. The estate was built in the early twentieth century. It seems like the gatehouse has hardly been touched since."

"So you walked into the kitchen . . ."

"Yes. I was juggling several parcels and trying not to drop the key while I closed the door behind me, so I didn't notice anything right away. Except there was an odd smell . . ." Her voice trailed away.

I knew it was better not to let her dwell on that. "Go on," I said sharply.

"I put the packages down on the table, and that's when I saw her." Claire closed her eyes briefly.

"Where was she?"

"Lying on the floor in the living room. At first, all I could see was Lila's lower legs and feet. The rest of her body was curled around the other side of this big upholstered chair. I thought maybe she'd tripped and fallen. I hoped she hadn't been seriously hurt." Claire looked stricken. "Can you imagine?"

"I know," I said quietly. "I know."

She braced herself and continued. "So I went to try and help her. I thought I could do that. How stupid of me. Because then I walked around the chair, and that's when I understood. Lila's eyes were open. There was a bullet hole in her chest. She was beyond anyone's help."

# Chapter
# Three

We sat in silence for a minute.

Then I asked, "What did you do next?"

"I screamed bloody murder," Claire retorted. "Then I backed up as fast as I could. I yanked out my phone and started calling for help."

A sudden knock on the side window of the compact car startled both of us. Claire and I jumped in our seats. I spun around and saw an unfamiliar face staring in at us.

The man was probably in his forties. He had bushy brown hair and what looked like a wiry build, now covered by several layers of clothing. His nose was broad, his cheeks were fleshy, and his lips were pursed. Judging by his expression, he was not happy.

Now that he had our attention, the man straightened and stepped away from the car. He beckoned impatiently with two fingers. He wanted us to get out. And to hurry up about it.

Detective Hronis, I assumed. It was a good thing I'd heard his name earlier, because he didn't bother to introduce himself.

"I thought I told you to wait over there," he said to Claire.

"Yes, but—"

"She was cold," I told him. "It's freezing out here. Didn't that occur to you before you went inside?"

His gaze swung my way. "Who are you?"

"Melanie Travis. Claire's sister," I added for good measure. I'd already told the lie once, so I figured I might as well run with it.

"What are you doing here?"

"Apparently, I'm looking out for my sister's welfare. Which is more than can be said for you. If Claire hadn't called emergency services, you wouldn't even be here. She was trying to be a good citizen and do the right thing—and look how she got treated in return. I understand that you need to talk to her, but you have no right to mistreat her while she waits for you to get around to doing it."

Hronis looked taken aback. He glanced over at the wooden bench, then back to the car. "Could be, you're right," he admitted, then turned to Claire. "Ms. Travis, you have my apologies. I should have thought that through before I left you sitting out here."

"Thank you," Claire replied. She sounded surprised.

That made two of us.

"Now if you don't mind, I'd like you to step inside so we can talk," he said. I saw Claire go still. Hronis must have noticed, too, because he added, "We'll go in through the front door. There's a small office on the other side of the cottage. My men are still working, but you won't able to see a thing from there. I promise."

Claire looked shaky, but she nodded.

"I'm coming too," I said.

Hronis held up a hand. He looked ready to argue. Then he glanced at Claire and changed his mind. "You can come," he told me. "But only if you stay out of the way and keep your mouth shut. This is her story, and I want to hear it in her own words. You got that?"

"I've got it," I confirmed. I was happy to remain quiet— just as long as Claire didn't say anything that might get her in trouble.

Normally, I wouldn't have been worried about that. Claire was smart and had plenty of common sense. I'd never seen a sticky situation she couldn't talk her way out of. But today's circumstances were far from normal. And ever since I'd arrived, everything about Claire had radiated uncertainty.

So although I'd told Detective Hronis that I would stay out of the way, I grasped her hand and gave it a firm squeeze. I made sure that my shoulder was level with hers as we walked around to the front of the gatehouse. And when she strode through the front door, I was mere inches behind her.

The detective preceded us through the doorway and immediately took a hard right. Eyes cast downward, Claire quickly followed.

I had only a few seconds to gaze around the interior of the cottage before doing the same. The dwelling appeared to consist of just a few rooms. I glimpsed a stone fireplace in the hallway and an artfully decorated Christmas tree in the living room. Other than that, there wasn't much to see.

The furniture inside the home was shabby, and the floorboards were warped beneath my feet. The wallpaper in the hall looked as though it might have dated from the middle of the previous century. There was an old water stain on the ceiling.

It occurred to me that someone who could afford to hire Claire to do her Christmas shopping should also have been able to afford to upgrade her furnishings. The gatehouse was part of the larger estate, however. I supposed that meant it was a rental. Probably everything inside had come with it.

Once we'd entered the small office, Detective Hronis closed the door behind us. He stepped over to the window and pushed aside a pair of heavy damask drapes. The weak winter light that filtered down through the trees around the gatehouse didn't help much.

Someone had placed two ladder-back chairs so that they were facing each other in the center of the room. A third was pushed against a wall. I thought about moving it to join the others, then decided against it. I'd be able to see and hear everything from where it was.

I unbuttoned my coat and pulled it off. I unwound my scarf, then tossed both items on a narrow bench nearby. Claire did the same. Her hat followed. She shook out her long hair. It rippled down to the middle of her back.

The detective watched us get comfortable. He unfastened his overcoat but left it on. When we were ready, he waved us both to our seats. As Claire sat down, she shivered slightly and crossed her arms over her chest.

"Are you warm enough now?" Hronis asked her.

"Yes, thank you. I'm fine," she replied. The answer was automatic. Seconds later she amended it. "Well, not fine. But I'm okay."

"Good. Then let's begin. What was your connection to the deceased woman, Lila Moran?"

"She was a client of mine," Claire said. "I like to think we were becoming friends."

"Ms. Moran hired you to do something for her?"

"That's correct." She briefly outlined the scope of her services. I was happy to see that Claire was keeping her answers short and to the point. That would give the detective less opportunity to trip her up.

"It sounds to me as if you hadn't known her very long," he said.

"No, we first met about a month ago. Some people wait until the last minute to think about Christmas shopping. But Lila was super organized. She wanted to have everything finished in plenty of time, so she could enjoy the holiday without having to worry about it."

"And that's why she employed you?"

"Yes." Claire nodded. "That's why all my customers employ me. I do the worrying for them."

Hronis shifted in his chair. I didn't blame him. The hard wooden seats could have used a cushion.

"How did Ms. Moran find out about your services?" he asked. "Would that have been in response to an advertisement you ran?"

"Some people do come to me that way," Claire agreed. "Others find me on Facebook or Instagram. In Lila's case, a friend of hers for whom I'd planned a children's party recommended me to her."

"I see," he replied. "Is that unusual?"

"Not at all. Anyone who works for himself will tell

you that good word of mouth is the best recommendation you can get. I love when former customers bring me repeat business or send me new clients."

Claire glanced over at me and smiled. Due to my connections at Howard Academy, I'd sent several customers to her myself. Hronis observed the exchange with interest. Evidently he didn't miss much.

"Let's move on to today's events," he said. "What brought you to Ms. Moran's house this morning?"

"I had a delivery to make." Claire had already indicated that was one of the services she offered. "Lila told me she expected to be working late tonight and she wouldn't have time to pick up the presents I'd bought for her. One was for a Christmas party she planned to attend this weekend. I offered to drop everything off to make sure she got it in time."

"Those were the wrapped packages that are sitting on the kitchen table?" the detective asked.

"That's right."

"So if I'm understanding this correctly, when you arrived you expected the house to be empty?"

"Yes."

"You intended to come inside, drop off your parcels, and leave. Is that right?"

Claire nodded. And frowned. I could understand why. It sounded to me as though she was being made to answer every question twice.

"But you didn't do that," the detective said.

"No. I did not."

"Why not?"

"Because as soon as I put the packages down on the table, I could see . . ." Claire stopped speaking. She waved a hand in the air ineffectually. "I could see . . ."

"What did you see?" Hronis prompted.

Claire had been sitting up straight, but now her body slumped. She blinked rapidly several times. Suddenly she looked as though she might cry.

I started to rise. But then a slight shake of Claire's head made me settle back in my seat—not happily. "Is this really necessary?" I asked the detective.

He nailed me with a hard look. "If it wasn't, we wouldn't be here." His voice gentled as he turned back to Claire. "Think back, Ms. Travis. What exactly did you see?"

"I saw Lila's feet," she said slowly. "And her lower legs. I thought maybe she had tripped. Or fallen."

"Did you notice anything else?"

"No. Not until . . ." She sighed. "Not until I stepped around the chair. I thought I might be able to help her."

"What did you do then?"

"I backed away very quickly and called for help."

Hronis leaned forward in his seat. "Did you touch Ms. Moran?"

"No." Claire shook her head vehemently. "I did not."

"And yet you knew she was dead."

"There was . . ." Her hand came up and flapped in the air again. "There was a lot of blood."

"I see." The detective paused, as if he was gathering his thoughts. I suspected he already knew exactly what he was going to say next. "You told the dispatcher that there had been an accident at this address."

"Did I?" Claire asked. "I don't remember."

"You did," he said. "What was it about the scene you saw that made you believe it was an accident?"

"I don't think I really did believe that. I was upset, and probably babbling. It was the first thing I thought to say.

Because the alternative was just too horrible to contemplate. All I wanted was for someone—anyone—to come and help."

Detective Hronis nodded, as if acknowledging that her reply made sense. "Just a few more questions," he said.

I glanced at my watch. I was surprised to see that the two of them had been talking for nearly half an hour.

"How familiar are you with Ms. Moran's home?" he asked.

"Excuse me?" said Claire.

"How many times had you been here previously?"

"Twice," Claire answered without hesitation. "Once when Lila and I initially met and she agreed to hire me, and then a second time when I had other presents to drop off."

"Nothing other than that? Maybe when the two of you got together socially?"

"No," Claire replied.

"Even though Ms. Moran was someone you felt you were beginning to think of as a friend?"

"Detective," I broke in before Claire could speak. There was a warning note in my tone. "What is this about?"

He held up his hands in front of him, a protest of innocence. I wasn't fooled for a minute. I doubted Claire was either. Detective Hronis was fishing for something. Perhaps trying to get Claire to admit to a deeper relationship than she and Lila had actually possessed.

"I'm just wondering whether or not Ms. Travis might have noticed anything that was different about the house on this visit," he said. "Maybe something that had been moved or was out of place. That's all."

*All*, my foot.

"I wouldn't know about that," Claire replied frostily.

She stood up. "I've already told you everything I know. Are we finished?"

"Almost," the detective said. He remained seated as she walked over to the bench where her outerwear lay. "Just one last thing."

Claire picked up her hat and jammed it on her head. "What's that?"

"When you arrived here this morning, you entered through the back door."

"That's correct."

"Was the door open or closed when you got here?"

"Closed. I had to juggle the packages into one arm so I could turn the knob."

The detective tipped his head to one side, considering. "It wasn't locked, then?"

"Yes, the door was locked when I arrived. I knew where to find the key."

"You knew where to find the key," he repeated slowly. Meaningfully. "Even though you'd only been here twice before?"

"Look," Claire said firmly. "Lila knew I was coming this morning. And she certainly didn't want—or expect—me to leave her nice presents sitting outside on the stoop. She told me to let myself in and put them on the kitchen table."

"Inside the house," Hronis said. "With the key."

"No," I snapped. "With a sledgehammer."

I got up and grabbed my coat too. I was *so* ready to be done with this.

"You're not helping," he growled at me.

I gave him a look that said the feeling was mutual. Just so we understood each other.

Detective Hronis finally rose to his feet. He was taller

than both of us, and he seemed to enjoy having that height advantage. He gazed down at Claire and said, "Something terrible happened here. Since you knew Ms. Moran, I would think you'd want to help us get to the bottom of things. Anything you might know, or suspect, or that you're even wondering about—no matter how small or insignificant—now would be the time to speak up."

Claire did him the courtesy of thinking about it before she replied. "No," she said finally. "I'm sorry I can't be more helpful, but I've said everything I have to say."

"You're sure about that?"

I rolled my eyes, but Claire managed a second civil answer.

"Yes, I'm sure."

"All right." The detective sounded resigned. "We're going to need you to stop by the police station to get fingerprinted. If you could take care of it this morning, that would be best."

Claire's body stilled. She looked shocked. Clearly she hadn't expected that. "Am I a suspect, Detective Hronis?"

"Right now, all I can tell you is that we'll be investigating every possible connection we see." He walked over to the door and opened it. "I trust the fingerprinting won't be a problem?"

Claire tossed her head. Then she preceded him through the doorway. "No, it won't be a problem."

She left the house without looking back. I paused before following her.

"I hope you find whoever did this," I said to the detective.

"Don't worry," he told me. "We will." He slipped a hand in his pocket and pulled out a business card. "If your sister thinks of anything else she wants to talk about, tell her to call me at this number."

That didn't seem likely, but I took the card anyway.

I'd intended to catch up with Claire but by the time I walked out the front door of the gatehouse, her Civic was already heading down the driveway toward the road. When Claire reached Forest Glen, she turned the car in the direction of town and sped away.

I stood and stared after her. That was odd. She was the one who'd asked me to come. So why hadn't she waited so we could leave together?

I hoped it wasn't a bad sign that Claire had been in such a hurry to escape.

# Chapter
# Four

Unbelievably, after all that, I was still on schedule to swing by Graceland Nursery School and pick up Kevin before heading home. With everything that had transpired since I'd left earlier that morning, it felt like it ought to be at least dinner time.

I spent the trip back to Stamford brooding about Claire's precipitous departure from the Mannerly estate. And wondering if there was more to the situation, and perhaps to her relationship with Lila Moran, than she had wanted to let on.

But those thoughts vanished as soon as Kev saw my car and quickly separated himself from the rest of the children who were waiting in front of the school. I imme-diately switched gears and turned into Mom again. It was a relief to be able to let everything else go—at least for the time being.

My younger son was four and a half, going on twelve. He had floppy blond hair, two skinned knees, and boundless energy. His body seemed to be made of equal parts rubber and lightning. Kevin asked more questions than I knew how to answer, and gave the best hugs of anyone I knew.

As he came racing toward the car, I got out and I waved to the two teachers who were supervising school dismissal. Kevin threw open the Volvo's back door and hopped into his car seat. He buckled himself in while I got his backpack settled on the floor at his feet. I checked the belts he'd fastened, then hurried around to the driver's seat. Preschool pick up was busy. There was already a line of cars forming behind us.

"How was school?" I asked once we were underway.

"Great!" Kevin crowed. Pretty much everything makes him happy.

Before we'd even left the school property, he was already gazing out the side window. Red cars are his favorite. He likes to count how many we pass on the road.

"What did you do today?"

"We're working on Christmas presents. One!" Kev pointed as a red Mazda went speeding by.

"That's nice. What are you making?"

"It's a secret." He laughed. "I can't tell."

"Who are you making them for?"

"Mo-om." He groaned. "That's a secret too."

"Okay." I glanced back over my shoulder. "I thought you and I could work on putting together another frame for Davey this afternoon. You know, since Bud ate the first one."

Kevin had come up with the idea to make his brother a customized picture frame for Christmas. He'd envisioned one that was the right size to hold the win picture commemorating Davey's last dog show with Augie—the one where the Standard Poodle had finished his championship. The plan was to take a plain wooden frame and glue dog biscuits all around the outer edge for decoration.

I'd thought that was a wonderful idea—until Bud had sniffed out our half-finished project and helped himself to all the edible parts, destroying the remainder of the frame in the process. Now we needed to buy new supplies and start over. And find a better hiding place.

"Two!" Kevin crowed. This time it was a pickup truck.

"What do you think?" I asked. "Should we stop at the crafts store?"

"Sure. Look, three!"

Four and a half is a great age. Everything is just that easy.

Life stopped being easy as soon as we got home an hour later. That was when I found out that Aunt Peg was coming to dinner.

"Did we invite her?" I asked Sam.

"We didn't have to," he informed me. "She invited herself."

It figured.

"Peg said she'd wasted half the morning waiting for you to call her," Sam mentioned. He was holding our packages from the craft store as Kevin and I stood in the front hall, shedding our outerwear.

I hung up my winter coat in the closet. Sam deftly

nabbed Kev's mittens before they hit the floor. The Poodles were waiting for us to finish. Those dogs were all opportunists. They knew I felt guilty for leaving them, and that meant everyone would get a biscuit.

"As you might imagine, that came as a surprise to me." Sam slanted a look in my direction. "Since I thought the two of you were together. When you didn't get back to her, Peg decided to take matters into her own hands. She's coming over to find out for herself what's going on."

"Oh," I said. I had forgotten to call Aunt Peg. Possibly on purpose.

Sam followed me to the kitchen. "That 'oh' sounds like the beginning of a story."

My husband knows me well. In my life, there's almost always a story. And this one was a doozy.

"Claire called while I was at Aunt Peg's house," I said as I handed out the dog biscuits, one to a customer, with an extra scratch under the chin for Faith.

"Mom was playing with puppies," Kevin told him. I'd filled him in on that part on the way home. "They have silly names."

"Larry, Moe, and Curly?" asked Sam.

I was pretty sure Kev didn't know who the Three Stooges were. He giggled anyway. "No! They're Black, Blue, and Ditto."

Sam grinned. "With names like that, it sounds like she doesn't intend for them to be around for long." When it mattered, Aunt Peg was all about finding the perfect name for a new puppy. "How's Claire doing?"

"She's had better days," I replied, frowning. "So have I."

I looked at Kev meaningfully. Sam got the hint.

"Hey squirt, why don't you run up to your bedroom

and find a book for us to read?" he said. "Take your time. Pick out something really good."

"Okay." Kevin's eyes lit up. He loves to pretend he knows how to read. "Come on, Bud. You can help." The two of them went flying out of the room.

Sam waited until Kev was out of earshot, then said, "I'd give him two minutes. Three, if we're lucky. Talk fast."

So I did. I summarized what had happened first. Then I summarized what I knew about the morning's events. That part didn't take very long, because I didn't know much. I was already running out of useful things to say when Kevin and Bud returned.

Kev was holding out a battered copy of *Go, Dog. Go!* Really, I should have seen that coming.

"I'm ready," he said, thrusting the book at Sam. "I'll read the first page. Then it's your turn."

So we tabled the rest of our discussion for later.

Davey's school bus dropped him off at the end of the driveway at four o'clock. When he walked in the back door, he was looking down at his phone. Davey had turned fourteen in September and had shot up in height around the same time. He had my first husband's lean build, and also his dark brown eyes. He glanced up at me as he kicked out a foot to shut the door behind him.

"Did you know Aunt Peg is coming for dinner?" he asked. "She says she's bringing barbecue from that new place that just opened up in Cos Cob."

"You're texting with Aunt Peg?"

I was standing in the middle of the kitchen. Kevin and I had just finished working on Davey's present. Kev had run upstairs to hide the frame in the back of his closet. I was cleaning up the supplies we'd used. Quickly I shoved the glue out of sight in a nearby drawer.

"Sure." Davey held up the screen. "See?"

"I didn't know Aunt Peg knew how to text."

"Everybody knows how to text." He dropped his backpack on a chair and headed straight for the refrigerator. "Except you."

"I know how," I informed him loftily. "I just choose not to. I would rather talk to someone. Conversation is a dying art."

"Yeah." Davey smirked. "Hold that thought." He grabbed a banana and disappeared.

Aunt Peg showed up at six o'clock. "I was going to wait until a more fashionable hour. But this barbecue smelled too good not to eat right away. I hope everybody's hungry."

She shoved two large parcels into my arms, then stooped down to say hello to the Poodles, who were swarming around her legs eagerly. As usual, they greeted her like a long-lost savior. From what, I wasn't entirely sure. Most days, I'm pretty sure those dogs have a better life than I do.

Bud refused to join the fray. Instead, he stood off to one side, keeping a beady eye on the food. The little dog had been half starved when he came home with us. Now he never missed a meal.

Davey's head popped over the railing on the second floor landing. "Do I smell brisket?" he asked.

"You most certainly do." Aunt Peg looked up at him, and Eve took the opportunity to lick her neck. "Along with pulled pork, baked beans, coleslaw, and corn bread. Enough for everyone to have an enormous helping."

Davey came bounding down the steps. "You ought to come to dinner more often."

"Someone ought to invite me more often," Aunt Peg said crisply. She braced a hand on her knee and rose to her feet as Sam and Kev came around the corner from the living room.

"I'm pretty sure you have a standing invitation," Sam said. He sniffed the air, then grabbed the bags out of my arms. "But we don't need to haggle about that now. Let's eat."

The table was already set, and drinks were already poured. All we had to do was find our seats, open the containers, and dig in. By unspoken agreement, none of the adults brought up the topic that had brought Aunt Peg to our house until dinner was finished and the two boys had left the room.

Davey had homework to do. Before going upstairs, he set up a movie for his younger brother in the living room. I cleared the table while Sam brewed coffee for the two of us and heated water for Aunt Peg's Earl Grey tea. The Poodles were lying on the floor around us. They knew they didn't get leftovers from the table, but they remained ever hopeful that one night we'd relax the rules. I gave Faith a pat instead, and retook my seat.

"This is the point in the evening where you're supposed to offer me dessert," Aunt Peg said. "A piece of cake would do nicely."

"We don't have cake," Sam said. "How about an Oreo?"

She did not look amused.

"How about a recap of the day's events?" I offered.

Aunt Peg nodded. "That will suffice."

I told her everything that had happened after I'd left

her house and gone rushing to New Canaan. Sam had already heard an abbreviated version of the story and I meant to give Aunt Peg the same. But since she stopped me every few seconds to ask questions, the retelling expanded greatly in length.

"So who is this woman, Lila Moran?" she asked at the end. "What do we know about her?"

"Not very much," I replied. "Mostly just that she's a new client of Claire's."

"Age? Occupation? Marital status? Reason she doesn't do her own Christmas shopping?" Aunt Peg lobbed questions at me faster than I could shake my head.

"If you want all those answers, you should be talking to Claire," I said, exasperated.

"I would be—if I hadn't assumed that you'd already done so. From the sound of it, the two of you were together for more than an hour. It didn't occur to you to request some pertinent facts?"

"We were busy," I hedged. "And then the moment we weren't, Claire was gone."

"Gone where?" asked Sam.

"I wish I knew. One minute we were talking to Detective Hronis, and the next Claire had disappeared. I'd thought we'd walk out together, maybe compare notes about the interview. But the detective stopped me to give me his card, and before I could get away, Claire had left. It was almost as though she couldn't wait to escape."

"How very unexpected." Aunt Peg frowned.

"I thought so too. Claire merely had a business relationship with the woman. It was just bad luck that she was the one to discover the body." I looked back and forth between Sam and Aunt Peg. "It's not as though she could have anything to hide. *Is there*?"

"It seems to me that ought to be the first thing you find out," Aunt Peg said.

"Tell us more about the place where Lila Moran lived," said Sam. "You called it a gatehouse?"

"Yes. It's a cottage situated just inside the entrance to a very large estate. I can't imagine who would own a place that looks like that. The property is really overgrown, and the gatehouse is decrepit. It's kind of creepy."

"Creepy?" Aunt Peg perked up. She loved anything that sounded mysterious.

"Everything looked neglected. The outer edge of the estate is like a wild forest. Nobody's pruned back those trees in years. Even in winter, the branches are thick enough to block the light from getting through. The whole place gave me an eerie feeling."

"Or maybe it was the dead body that did that," Sam murmured.

"Even a small home in New Canaan costs a bundle," Aunt Peg mused. "It seems odd that someone would let a property that size fall to ruin. Did the place have a name?"

"Claire referred to it as the Mannerly estate."

"Mannerly?" Aunt Peg's eyes widened. She sat up suddenly. "As in Josephine Mannerly?"

"Could be." I shared a glance with Sam. Neither one of us knew who she was talking about. "The name fits."

"Well then, I suppose *that* would explain a few things."

"Who's Josephine Mannerly?" Sam asked.

"Really?" She stared at the two of us. "You've never heard of her?"

We figured that was a hypothetical question. We both declined to answer.

Aunt Peg's gaze moved past us to Faith and Eve, who were sleeping side by side on the floor. Their bodies were aligned from the tops of their heads to the bases of their tails. "One might think the Poodles have a better grasp of local history than my own relatives do."

"And one might be right," I conceded.

I stood up and went to pour myself a second cup of coffee. It wasn't decaf. That probably meant that I'd be up all night. But caffeine made my brain work better. And when Aunt Peg was conducting an interrogation, I needed to keep my wits about me.

I lifted the pot and tilted it in Sam's direction. He shook his head. Smart man.

I'd barely sat back down at the table before Aunt Peg said, "Josephine Mannerly was the most stunning debutante ever to make her debut at the Grosvenor Ball."

I swiveled in my seat in surprise. "You *knew* her?"

"Many, many, years ago our families socialized in the same circles, so we were slightly acquainted with one another. I was several years younger than Josie, but that didn't matter. Everyone in my set knew who she was."

Reminiscing made Aunt Peg smile. "It wasn't as if we had a choice. Our mothers pointed Josie out to us. They extolled her grace and feminine virtues. For those of us who might have been inclined toward hoydenish behavior, Josie was held up as a model of ladylike comportment."

I bit back a smile. It didn't surprise me in the slightest that Aunt Peg had been known as a young hoyden. Apparently little had changed in the intervening decades.

"Josie's father had scads of money," she continued. "I believe most of it came from copper mines and railroads. When the Second World War broke out, he was too old to serve but like many men of his generation, he signed up anyway. Tragically, he was killed in France when Josie was barely a toddler."

Aunt Peg sighed. "I don't think Josie's mother ever recovered from the loss. The family was living in the city at the time—eighteen rooms on Park Avenue, if I remember correctly. Back then, the estate in New Canaan was merely a weekend retreat. Over the next two decades, Ada Mannerly immersed herself in the New York social whirl, and that meant Josie did too. Josie was an only child, and Ada's life revolved around her."

"That doesn't sound like a good thing," I said.

"I'd imagine it wasn't," Aunt Peg agreed. "Especially since the society pages chronicled their every move. I doubt that Josie enjoyed even a modicum of privacy during her teenage years. And of course, the reporters called her a poor little rich girl. Then, to everyone's dismay, that proved to be oddly prescient."

"What happened?" asked Sam. He was listening to the story just as avidly as I was.

"It was only a year or so after Josie made her debut that tragedy struck again. Her mother drowned in a boating accident off Nantucket. Josie had barely turned twenty at the time. The relationship she had with her mother had been her whole world, and then suddenly her mother was gone too. Josie disappeared after that."

"Disappeared?" I gulped. "What do you mean?"

"Josie withdrew from society," Aunt Peg replied. "She stopped going out. She refused to take her friends' calls. She abandoned the New York apartment and moved to Connecticut. Aside from the servants, she lived all alone in that big house and saw no one. It was as though she'd fled from everyday life."

"That must have been fifty years ago," Sam said wonderingly.

"Nearly half a century," Aunt Peg agreed. "Once upon a time, Josephine Mannerly was dubbed the Deb of the Decade. But to the best of my knowledge, nobody has seen or heard from her in years."

# Chapter
# Five

"Do you think she's still alive?" I asked.

"I don't see why not," Aunt Peg replied. "Surely the press would have reported on her death if she wasn't."

"Is she still living in that house?"

Aunt Peg stared at me across the table. "How would I know that?"

The question made me laugh. "You seem to know just about everything else about her."

"Oh pish," she said. "I was an impressionable young girl and Josie was being held up to me as a paragon, a living example of everything I was meant to strive for. So of course I studied her closely. But that was decades ago. All the information I have about her is sadly out of date now. Not only that, but I hadn't given her a thought in years until *you* brought her up."

"Strictly speaking, I only mentioned her estate," I pointed out.

"*And* jogged my memory," Aunt Peg shot back.

"Stop squabbling you two." Sam held up a hand for silence. "You're both overlooking the most important question. Considering who Josephine Mannerly is, what was Lila Moran doing in her gatehouse?"

"Presumably, living there," I said. "Possibly renting it."

"Yes, but why?" Sam persisted. "Why would a very wealthy woman, one who's lived as a recluse for years, allow that? Why would she want anyone in there?"

"You're right, that is puzzling," Aunt Peg agreed. "We need to find out more about Lila Moran. Who she was, and where she came from."

"Or we need to let the police hunt down that information," I said.

"Don't be ridiculous. It's not as though they're going to tell us what they find out. We should do a little snooping around on our own."

Of course she would say that.

"And I know just the place for you to start," Aunt Peg added with satisfaction. "Isn't it handy that we have someone right in our own family who can answer our questions? You need to talk to Claire and find out what she knows."

For once, Aunt Peg and I were in full agreement. I did need to talk to Claire. And Aunt Peg's questions weren't the only ones I had.

I understood why Claire had called me when she'd discovered Lila Moran's body in the gatehouse. I have an uncanny tendency to stumble upon unfortunate situations myself. So I can see why someone might think I possess useful experience in that regard.

So I'd been happy to drop what I was doing—playing with puppies, let's not forget!—and dash to Claire's side. I'd been ready to offer whatever kind of help or support was needed. I'd even been prepared to run interference between Claire and the authorities.

What I hadn't expected was to find myself standing alone on that cold driveway, watching Claire flee—as though now that I'd served my purpose, she couldn't get away from me fast enough.

That demanded an explanation. And it had better be good.

The next morning I called Claire and told her we had to talk. She told me to meet her at the Stamford Town Center. Considering the conversation I wanted to have, that location wouldn't have been my first choice.

Stamford Town Center was a large shopping mall downtown. It had seven levels and more than a hundred stores, which were wrapped around a central atrium. The place was bright, and noisy, and fun. On a normal day, it attracted shoppers from all over Fairfield County.

So I could picture what the mall would look like now, in mid-December. With just three weeks until Christmas, the place would be a veritable madhouse—which Claire must have known. If she hoped that threatening to drag me to that holiday shopping mecca would permit her to avoid me again, she'd need to rethink her plan. I was made of sterner stuff than that.

We'd arranged to meet at Barnes & Noble, on the fourth level. The exterior of the store was draped in pine roping and twinkled with fairy lights. Christmas music played quietly in the background. When I stepped inside the wide entrance, Claire was already there.

Browsing through a selection of bestsellers on a front table, she looked up and smiled as I approached. Claire was wearing a white merino wool tunic, paired with burgundy leggings. There were suede booties on her feet, and some professional had done amazing things to her eyebrows.

I had on jeans and sneakers. The puffy down jacket I'd worn outside was now slung over my arm. I'd brushed my hair that morning before running out to drop Kevin off at preschool, and I'd meant to put on lipstick.

It was kind of funny to realize that the same man had managed to marry both of us.

"Books," I said, nodding toward the table. "Someone has good taste. Are you shopping for yourself or a client?"

"Oh, please. Do you even have to ask?" she said with a grin. "I'm like the cobbler whose children have no shoes. I'll be lucky if I have time to fit in my own shopping on Christmas Eve. I need a present for a quiet ten-year-old boy. His mother wanted a Nerf gun. I suggested a book on astronomy."

"Looks like you won," I said.

"We're compromising. He's getting both. Come on, the children's section is in the back. I'm sure I'll be able to find something there."

The Claire who'd just greeted me was aeons away from the shell-shocked woman I'd spent time with the previous morning. Perhaps her hasty departure had had nothing to do with me. Maybe she'd simply been eager to put the whole distressing episode behind her. Even so, it seemed surprising that less than twenty-four hours later, Claire appeared to have nothing more weighty on her mind than the need to search for perfect gifts.

It took us less than ten minutes to locate just the right book. Claire declined an offer of gift wrapping and placed the purchase in her roomy tote. Over the next hour, I followed her from one store to the next. I watched as she examined goods ranging from alpaca scarves to cell phone chargers and Swiss Army knives.

"Sorry I'm so busy," Claire said as she hopped on an escalator to travel to an upper level. "I guess this isn't what you hoped to be doing when you said we should get together."

I stepped on after her. "The point wasn't to get together. I want us to talk about yesterday."

Claire sighed. "There isn't much to say. You were there. You know what happened."

"Not everything. I still have questions."

She spun around to look at me. "You *always* have questions." Her tone sounded almost accusing.

Claire wasn't paying attention, and she stumbled slightly when we reached the next level and the stairs flattened beneath us. Quickly she caught herself and found her footing. She strode away.

"If that annoys you, you shouldn't have asked me to help," I said to her retreating back.

Claire's steps slowed. Then stopped. We were standing in the line of traffic beside a display of giant candy canes. Harried shoppers dodged around us. Half of them were on their phones. All were intent on their own problems. No one paid attention to us.

A loudspeaker somewhere was piping out "Joy to the World." Not so much where I was standing.

Claire's shoulders stiffened. She turned to face me. "You're saying this is *my* fault?"

"No," I replied calmly. "I'm saying that we need to talk."

"Does it have to be now?"

I shrugged. "That's the only reason I'm here."

An elf popped his head out of the candy cane display. He said to Claire, "For Pete's sake, lady, just talk to her, wouldja? Maybe then she'll leave you alone." The elf looked at me. "Right?"

"Right," I agreed. At this point I'd take help anywhere I could get it—even from a guy with pointy shoes and bells on his cap.

Claire lifted a finger and pointed. "Upstairs."

"We just came up," I said.

"There's a food court up there," the elf told me helpfully. "Maybe she's cranky because she's hungry."

"Maybe she's cranky because she wants both of you to butt out," Claire snapped back.

"See?" He waggled a finger. "Cranky. Feed her. It'll help. Trust me, I know these things."

Neither one of us said a word until we were on the next escalator heading upward. Then, to my surprise, Claire suddenly dissolved in a fit of giggles. "Trust me," she mimicked, "I know these things. Poor guy. I guess Mrs. Elf must be hard to live with."

"Hey, don't knock it," I said. "We're taking his advice, aren't we?"

"I guess." Her good humor vanished as quickly as it had come. "Are you really going to make me relive what happened yesterday?"

"Not all of it," I told her. "I just want to go over a few things."

The frozen yogurt stand was selling cups of raspberry whipped yogurt topped with chocolate chips. Claire and I each bought a double. It was still early, so the food court wasn't mobbed. We were able to find a small table overlooking the atrium.

Down below in the center of the mall, children were running and playing in a life-size gingerbread house. Despite the distance, we could hear their delighted shrieks of laughter. Giant holiday ornaments hung from shiny ribbons attached to the ceiling above us. Everywhere I looked, people were feeling festive.

Christmas was in the air. Except perhaps at our small table.

I dipped my spoon into my frozen yogurt and savored the first bite. "This is good."

"Of course it's good," Claire replied. "It's probably made of sugar." She peered down at the cup as if she was hoping to see a list of ingredients. "And possibly artificial flavor and food coloring."

"It's yogurt," I grumbled. She was raining on my parade. "That means it's practically health food."

"Uh-huh. And Santa Claus is alive and well and living at the North Pole." Nevertheless, Claire ate another spoonful. "You're the one who wanted to talk. I'm here. I'm listening. Have at it."

So much for chitchat. And on to the main event.

"Tell me about Lila Moran," I said.

"What about her?"

"Start with anything you happen to know. Where did she come from?"

Claire stopped and thought. "I don't believe Lila was a Connecticut native. At any rate, she was living in Massa-

chusetts before she came here. She'd been in New Canaan
for about a year."

"Why did she move here?"

"She took a job in Stamford. Officer manager for an
advertising agency. James and Brant?"

I shook my head. I hadn't heard of them, but that didn't
mean much. "And you met through a mutual friend?"

"That's right. Karen Clauson. Her husband works at
James and Brant too. They have three kids. I planned four
parties for them this year."

"Four?" I looked up.

"Three birthdays, plus an office function. Melanie,
what's this about?"

"I was talking to Aunt Peg last night—"

Claire groaned.

"Yeah, I know. But she was curious about Lila Moran
and so am I. It turns out that many years ago Aunt Peg
knew the woman who owns the estate where Lila was living."

"I don't know anything about that." Claire crunched a
chocolate chip with her teeth. "I never went any farther
inside than the gatehouse."

"Did you ever ask Lila how she came to be living
there?"

"No. Why would I?"

"Maybe because you were curious?" One could only
hope.

Claire shook her head. "Lila wasn't very chatty about
personal stuff. Although she did complain about the
place a couple of times. The furnace was iffy. A downstairs window was warped. I asked her why she didn't
get those things fixed, but she said it wasn't up to her.
There was a caretaker who was supposed to be looking

after the gatehouse, but he never got around to doing anything. That ticked her off pretty royally. She said once that she probably wouldn't be staying around much longer."

"And now she's dead," I said quietly.

When Claire grimaced, I regretted my blunt statement. It turned out that wasn't the problem.

"And I'm apparently a suspect," she retorted. "Which is utterly ridiculous. You heard what that detective said. They're investigating every connection. Even mine."

"Is that what you're so upset about?" I asked.

"I'm not upset," she shot back.

I helped myself to some more raspberry yogurt and waited her out.

"All right," Claire said after a minute. "I'm upset."

"I can tell," I said. "So talk to me. Do you have any thoughts about who might have wanted to harm Lila?"

"Of course not." She shoved another spoonful in her mouth. "Why would you even ask that?"

"Because you knew Lila and I didn't. And because you explained to me how your business worked. You would have talked with Lila about her friends and family. She'd have described the people she wanted you to buy presents for. Information that might be useful for Detective Hronis to have."

*"Useful."* Claire snorted. "You know that's Peg's favorite word."

I nodded. I did know that. Sometimes she referred to me as a useful person. It was supposed to be a compliment.

"Do you know something?" I prodded.

"Not about that," Claire said firmly. "Not even close. Think about it, Melanie. Who in their right mind would buy a Christmas present for someone who wanted to kill them?"

The question probably shouldn't have made me laugh, but it did. Even Claire managed a small smile.

"Then what?" I asked. "I know something's bothering you. And I don't have all day to hang around this mall, waiting for you to speak up. Come on, Claire, let's hear it."

"Has anyone ever told you that you're a giant pain in the posterior?"

"Sure. It happens all the time. Now spill."

Claire finished her last spoonful of yogurt. She pushed the cup to the side. "There is one thing."

Finally, we were getting somewhere. "What's that?"

"The woman who died yesterday in the gatehouse? I don't know who she was, but Lila Moran wasn't her real name."

# Chapter
# Six

"Shut the front door," I said.

Claire laughed at the expression on my face. "It's not often I manage to surprise you."

"Well, you've certainly done it now. What makes you think that?"

"A month ago, before the first time Lila and I got together, I did a background check on her."

She certainly had my attention. I leaned forward in my seat. "Why?"

"Because I'm a woman who runs my own business. And sometimes due to the nature of that business, I meet with clients alone in their homes. So mostly I do it for my own safety. You know, to make sure the people who want to hire me don't have any prior arrests or a history of past craziness. And of course, it also helps to know that when they contract my services, they actually have the money to pay me."

"I had no idea," I said admiringly. "I guess I should have. It only makes sense."

"Of course it does," she agreed.

"And what did Lila's background check reveal?"

"Not nearly enough." Claire frowned. "That was the problem."

"What do you mean?"

"With most people, in addition to that other stuff, you can also find out things like when and where they were born, their parents' names, and where they went to high school or college. You know, basic facts. But in Lila's case, none of that information existed."

I didn't get it. But then again, I'd never done a check on anyone. "How is that possible?"

"Good question. As far as I could tell, Lila Moran—the woman who was living in that gatehouse—came into existence about five years ago."

My eyes narrowed. "She made up a new identity."

"Something like that. Obviously I don't know for sure, but I'd never seen anything like it before."

"Did you ask her about it?" I demanded.

"No." Claire looked pained. "It didn't seem like it was any of my business."

"Not your business?" I repeated incredulously. "That's crazy. You ran a background check on a prospective client— and she flunked your query Big Time. Under those circumstances, why would you go to work for her?"

She winced at my tone but answered my query in a calm voice. "For starters, because Lila was recommended to me by someone I know and trust."

"The woman you mentioned earlier?"

"Yes, Karen Clauson. Not only is she a reputable person, but she and her husband are good clients too. So if I had turned Lila away without even meeting her, how would that have looked?"

"Gee, I don't know," I snapped. "Maybe like you were using your brain?"

Claire pushed back her chair and stood up. "You see? That's why I didn't want to tell you. I knew you'd think I'd done something stupid."

"Claire, I'm sorry." I blew out a breath. And felt like an utter ass. At least now I knew why she'd been avoiding me. "I shouldn't have said that. Please sit back down."

Reluctantly she did so. She folded her hands on the table and stared at me without saying anything. It was left to me to make amends.

"Okay," I said. "That was the first reason. Was there another?"

Claire nodded.

"Are you going to make me beg?"

"I'm thinking about it."

"How about if I go and get you another helping of frozen yogurt? Will that help?"

"My mood, yes." She smiled grudgingly. "My waistline, not in the slightest. The second reason was because once I'd met Lila, I found that I actually liked her. I mean, I knew there was something hinky about her background. But in person, she didn't seem like she was a deranged psychopath. Or indeed anything out of the ordinary at all. After I got to know her a bit, I even found myself trying to come up with reasons why she might have needed to become somebody else."

"Such as?"

"Maybe Lila was trying to escape from an abusive

husband," Claire told me seriously. "Or she could have been part of the witness protection program."

Both options sounded pretty far-fetched to me. But for Claire's sake, I was willing to play along. "I suppose those could be possibilities."

"You don't have to sound so skeptical. I would have asked her eventually, you know." Claire frowned. "I just thought I should wait until we had more of a relationship."

Now that would never happen. The depressing thought hung in the air between us. Claire hadn't just suffered the shock that came with finding a dead body. She'd also lost a friend.

"You should have told Detective Hronis about this," I said.

"No way," Claire replied. "He thinks of me as a suspect. I've watched enough episodes of *Law & Order* to know that unless you have a lawyer with you when you talk to the police, you should say as little as possible. And you especially shouldn't bring up something they might somehow find incriminating. Besides, the authorities have plenty of resources. By now, I'm sure they already know."

She was probably right about that.

Claire reached across the table, picked up my empty yogurt cup and spoon, and added them to her own. There was a trash container just behind us. She turned around and dumped everything in. People were standing around the edges of the food court waiting for tables. It was time for us to move on.

We both stood up. Claire gathered up her purse and the big tote. She checked something on her phone. "I still have two more stops to make. Are we good now?"

"We're good." I reached over and gave her a firm hug. "We're always good, even when we don't entirely see eye to eye."

"So what happens next?"

"What do you mean?"

"You're going to keep asking questions, aren't you?"

I wondered if it was my imagination that she sounded almost hopeful. "Do you want me to?"

Claire hesitated only briefly before nodding. "I hate this. It reminds me of last time." Her beloved brother had been murdered several years earlier. That tragic event had been the beginning of our relationship.

I was tempted to give her another hug, but Claire wasn't crumbling. Instead, her chin lifted defiantly.

"Plus," she said, "this kind of attention isn't good for my business."

"We can't have that," I agreed.

She pulled out her phone again and went to work. A minute later, she looked up. "I sent you Karen's contact info. She knew Lila better than I did. You should start with her."

When I got home, Sam was closeted in his office, working. So I grabbed the Poodles, plus Bud, and took the crew for a mile walk around the neighborhood. Our backyard was big and totally fenced in, and the dogs loved to hang out there. But aside from the occasional game of tag or tug-of-war, they rarely used it to exercise.

That was left to me. But what the heck. The walks were good for me too. And they gave me a chance to admire my neighbors' Christmas decorations.

The Standard Poodles knew how to listen, so they were

loose. Bud listened too—but then he was apt to make a unilateral decision to explore other options. So he was on a leash. When Raven and Eve saw something interesting a few houses away and dashed on ahead of us, the little dog looked up at me and whined.

"No," I said.

Bud wagged his tail hopefully.

"You know why."

He cocked his head to one side and gave me a doggy grin.

Dammit, he was adorable. I hardened my heart anyway. "Don't try to tell me you won't steal the baby Jesus from Mrs. DeLeo's crèche, because I know better. Last time, you dragged it all over her yard before I caught you, and I had to have his little gown dry cleaned."

Faith woofed under her breath. She'd enjoyed that.

Augie and Tar, busy peeing on every tree we passed, had lagged behind. Now the two male Poodles caught up with us. Surrounded once again by his buddies, Bud relaxed and we continued our walk.

Despite the lack of snow on the ground, the street looked ready for the holidays. Nearly all the houses had Christmas wreaths on their doors. Many had festive lights twined around their trees and bushes. One enterprising person had positioned a sleigh, with a blow-up Santa Claus and eight plastic reindeer, in the middle of his front yard. The neighborhood dogs had been barking at that for a week.

Sam and the boys had put up our outdoor lights a few days earlier, but we had yet to buy a wreath or a tree. That event was scheduled for the upcoming weekend when we planned to visit Haney's Holiday Home, a Christmas tree farm in Wilton owned by Bob and my brother, Frank.

Now in its second year of operation with them at the helm, the business was turning out to be an unexpected success.

When I returned from my walk, Sam and I had lunch together. Then I dashed out and picked up Kevin at preschool. When I called Karen Clauson after that, I found out that Claire had already smoothed the way for me. Not only did Karen know who I was, but she also said she'd be happy to speak with me.

"With three kids, I'm running around like crazy this time of year," she told me. "But I've got half an hour free this afternoon. Why don't you stop by?"

Karen also lived in Stamford so I told her I'd be there shortly. Leaving Sam in charge of the child and the dogs, I jumped back in the Volvo and quickly headed out.

Shippan Point was a small peninsula that jutted out into Long Island Sound in the southernmost part of the city. It was a neighborhood of large homes, yacht clubs, and private beaches. Karen and her husband, George, lived in a gracious three-story house with a large yard and views of the water.

A brisk breeze was blowing in off the Sound when I got out of my car in front of their home. I arranged my scarf more tightly around my neck and walked across the lawn. The cold air was bracing, but I still had to stop for a minute to appreciate the view. Even in winter, it was amazing.

I heard the front door open and looked up as a woman stepped out onto the wide porch. She was thin as a twig and had on leather boots and a cashmere turtleneck dress. A wide belt accentuated her enviably small waist. The woman's blond hair was gathered into a high ponytail that swung gently when the wind hit it.

She stood with her arms crossed over her chest, probably for warmth. Her hands pegged her as middle aged, but her face had the taut look of a much younger woman. As I went to join her, her smile was immediate and friendly. I could already understand why Claire liked her.

"I'm Karen," she said, extending a hand. "And you must be Melanie." She nodded toward the expanse of water, winter gray and rolling with whitecap-tipped waves. "It's beautiful, isn't it?"

"It certainly is," I agreed.

"Most people move here because they want to be near the shore in the summer. But I prefer this time of year, when everything looks so wild and untamed. It makes me feel small, like Mother Nature's making sure we understand who's actually in charge."

"I never thought about it that way before."

Karen laughed. "George says the same thing. He thinks I'm crazy. But as long as he can spend six months a year on his sailboat, he's willing to put up with frigid winters beside the Sound."

She had left the door open behind her and turned back to it now. "Let's go inside and warm up. I've got a fire burning in the living room. And there's a pot of coffee in the kitchen, if you'd like some."

"That sounds wonderful." I pulled off my coat and scarf and hung them on a coatrack near the door. "Thank you for agreeing to see me."

"As I'm sure you can imagine, Lila's death came as a huge shock to all of us. To tell you the truth, I'm happy to be able to talk about it with someone. The whole thing has left me feeling anxious, and even a bit jumpy. I just never expected to know someone who . . ." She stopped and cleared her throat softly. "This isn't the kind of place where you think something like that will happen."

I nodded. "I understand how you feel."

"Maybe this will sound morbid, but I keep thinking that if I can learn more about what took place, maybe that will help me to understand. I spoke with Claire briefly, but she sounded so fragile that I didn't want to press her for details. So when she told me that you were there with her yesterday . . ."

"You figured you'd get your questions answered while you were answering mine?" I asked.

"Yes, something like that. Let's get our coffee and sit down. We've got half an hour until my two youngest get home from school. We should put it to good use."

Karen's coffee was strong and hot, and the fire crackling in the fireplace gave the spacious living room a cozy feel. We found seats on two matching love seats that faced each other across a low butler's table.

"I understand you were the person who referred Lila Moran to Claire," I began.

"Yes, I was. Claire's done several events for us. Well, for me, really—George doesn't care a fig about the kids' birthday parties—and she's always done a phenomenal job. Whenever anyone asks for a recommendation, I'm always happy to send business her way."

"I'm sure Claire appreciates that."

"I'd imagine she did." Karen frowned. "Until this time."

"That was hardly your fault. I know Claire enjoyed working with Lila and getting to know her."

"Yes, she would have. Lila was like that. She made friends easily. She'd only been at James and Brant about a year, but she very quickly found her stride. It wasn't long before she fit right in."

"She was the officer manager there?" I asked.

"That's right."

"So you must have met Lila through your husband."

Karen blinked. She looked surprised by the question. "I guess I did; although not directly. James and Brant is an advertising firm. The principals like their people to be seen out and around, so George and I attend a number of functions each year. As soon as Lila joined the company, it was inevitable that our paths would begin to cross."

"How well did you know her?"

"I would say we were friends—which doesn't mean that we were particularly close. Lila and I led very different lives. I'm a stay-at-home mom and happy in that role. Lila was a career woman. She was ambitious, always keeping her eye out for the next opportunity. She never said as much to me, but I think she viewed the job at James and Brant as a stepping stone rather than an end destination."

My coffee had begun to cool. I picked it up and took a sip. "Claire didn't know much about Lila's background. Things like where she grew up or went to college. I was wondering if you know more?"

"Not really." Karen paused to consider. "I guess we never got around to talking about those things. George probably has that information. He's one of the partners in the firm. I'd be surprised if he didn't see her résumé before she was hired. I could ask him about it if you want."

"That would be great. Thank you." I appreciated that Karen was trying to be helpful, but it sounded as though she didn't know any more about Lila than Claire had.

In the fireplace a log snapped and fell, sending a spray

of sparks shooting into the air. Karen stood and picked up a pair of tongs. She rearranged the remaining wood to her satisfaction, then reached into a nearby bin and placed a new log on top of the pile. The flames quickly licked upward, seeking the fresh fuel.

"You look like an old hand at that," I said as she retook her seat.

"It's hard not to be when you live on the water in Connecticut. A toasty fire goes a long way toward taking the chill out of the air."

I nodded. She was right about that. "I know this is a difficult question. But do you have any thoughts about why someone might have wanted to harm Lila?"

"You mean kill her," Karen replied flatly.

"Yes."

"I heard she was shot."

"She was," I affirmed. "Do you know of any enemies she might have had?"

"None." Karen sighed. "That's what makes this whole situation so incomprehensible. I watch the news. I know that bad things happen. But I just never expected my family to be impacted by a violent crime like this. Please . . . tell me what happened. I heard Lila was found in her living room. Do you think she came home and interrupted a burglar?"

"I suppose that could have been the case." I considered that idea. "Although there didn't seem to be much in her home that anyone might have wanted to steal. And nothing else in the room looked as though it had been disturbed."

"Was the door locked when Claire got there? Do you think Lila admitted her killer to the house? Could it have been someone she knew?"

"Claire went in through the back door. She used a hidden key to let herself inside," I said. "I don't know whether or not the front door was locked—and maybe it wouldn't have mattered."

Karen looked up. "Why is that?"

"The gatehouse where Lila was living is pretty old. And it's seriously in need of upkeep. It didn't appear to be very secure."

"Oh," Karen said abruptly. "Oh my."

"What's the matter?" I asked.

"What you said just reminded me of something. It was a couple of months ago. With winter coming, Lila mentioned that her furnace needed to be repaired. I told her I could recommend someone. But she said there was a caretaker on the property who was supposed to do stuff like that. I said, 'Good, then you're all set,' but she shook her head and gave me the oddest look."

I sat up straight. "Did you ask why?"

"I did." Karen frowned, thinking back. "At first she didn't want to talk about it. But then she finally admitted that she was afraid of the guy. She didn't like him coming inside her house. Lila said he was convinced that she had something of his, something he wanted back. I didn't think any more about it at the time, but now I wonder. Do you think she was right to be worried?"

# Chapter
# Seven

"Yes," I said. Lila was dead. *Did she even have to ask?* "Have you talked to the police about that?"

"No." Karen appeared shocked by the suggestion.

"Because that sounds like useful information they should have."

She still didn't look convinced. "A detective showed up at James and Brant yesterday afternoon. George told me all about it. The detective talked to everyone. People who knew Lila much better than I did."

"But maybe they didn't know about this," I pointed out. "Was anyone else there when you and Lila had that conversation?"

"Let me think." Karen paused. "Yes, Chris was there. Chris Sanchez. She's one of the account reps. And she would have been at work yesterday. I'm sure she must have told the detective what Lila said."

I wasn't nearly as sure of that as she was. But Karen sounded so relieved to be off the hook that I decided not to press the issue.

"In fact," she said, standing up, "if you want to find out more about Lila, Chris is the person you should talk to. She and Lila have worked side by side for the past year. She would have known her better than I did."

Karen crossed the room to the desk in the corner. She opened a drawer and took out a pen and a sheet of paper. Then she got out her phone and wrote something down. "Here's her number. Call Chris. Tell her I sent you. I'm sure she'll be able to help you."

At least Chris would be able to tell me whether she'd passed along Lila's fear of the caretaker to the police. "Thanks," I said. "I appreciate it."

"Do you know what I think?" Karen asked as she accompanied me to the door. "That this was a totally random event. Like maybe Lila was just in the wrong place at the wrong time. And the police will catch the guy quickly so we can all put this behind us." She nodded firmly. "That's what's going to happen."

"I hope you're right," I said.


Shippan was in South Stamford. My house was in North Stamford. The offices for James and Brant were downtown, which meant I'd be driving virtually right past on my way home. So when I got out to my car, I took a shot and called Chris Sanchez.

It was mid-afternoon so I figured she'd be at work. If I

was lucky, maybe she'd be able to spare a few minutes to talk to me.

Chris sounded wary when she answered her phone. Since she hadn't recognized my number, she probably thought I wanted to sell her something. She thawed slightly when I introduced myself, and by the time I told her that Karen had put me in touch, Chris had become positively chatty. When I asked if I could stop by the office, she had another idea ready.

"Don't come here," she said. "There's a Starbucks on the corner. I can meet you there in fifteen minutes. Would that work?"

"That's perfect," I told her. "But I don't want to drag you away from things you're supposed to be doing."

"Don't worry about that. I'm happy to take a break. This place is a madhouse today. Of course, Lila's murder came as a huge shock to everyone. But her loss impacts us on a practical level, too, because suddenly we're without an office manager. Nobody will even notice if I duck out for a few minutes."

I beat her to the coffee shop, picked up a caffè mocha, and grabbed a table. Chris came flying in two minutes later. She looked to be in her early thirties. Her skin was lightly freckled, and her dark hair was gathered into a messy bun on the top of her head. She'd run out of the office without bothering to put on a coat, which probably accounted for her speed.

Chris paused just inside the door and took a look around. I was the only single woman sitting alone, so she gave me a small wave. I waved back and smiled. She stopped at the counter to buy an espresso and a slice of lemon pound cake.

As she slipped into a chair opposite me, Chris set the cake plate and two forks on the table between us. "This is big enough to share. And that way I only have to worry about half the calories. I hope you're Melanie, otherwise I am offering sweets to a total stranger. And that could probably get me in trouble."

"Yes, I'm Melanie," I said with a laugh. "And I never mind when someone offers me cake. Thank you for agreeing to talk to me."

"Hey, like I said, it was a good excuse to escape the mayhem." She was already digging into the pound cake. "How do you know Karen?"

"Actually, we just met earlier. She and I were talking about what happened to Lila Moran."

Chris looked up. "Why?"

"Because I was at Lila's house yesterday morning, after her body was discovered."

"Oh." Chris took a swallow of her espresso. "So are you some kind of plainclothes cop or something? Because we talked to those guys yesterday."

"No. Claire Travis, the woman who found Lila, is a good friend of mine. She was in a panic, and she called and asked me to come and help."

"Claire Travis." Chris stared at me. "And you're Melanie Travis?"

I nodded.

"Friends, not relatives?"

"Claire is married to my ex-husband," I said.

She barked out a laugh. "How's that working out?"

"Surprisingly well."

"I guess so." Chris shook her head. She looked bemused. "Considering that you were the one she called, and now you're here talking to me. Is Claire the personal shopper?"

"That's right."

Chris helped herself to another piece of cake. At this rate, I wouldn't get a single bite. "Lila mentioned her the other day. The rest of us were complaining about all the Christmas shopping we still had to do, and Lila started bragging that she was already finished. So of course we wanted to know how she'd managed that. Made me think I should consider trying it next year."

"Claire does a great job." I was always happy to give her a plug.

"Except that her client is dead," Chris mentioned.

"That's not Claire's fault."

"You sure about that?"

"Of course I'm sure." I huffed out a breath.

She lifted her head and studied me. "Even though she stole your husband?"

The accusation was so absurd that it made me laugh. "Claire didn't steal my husband. Bob and I had been divorced for years before the two of them even met."

"Maybe that's just what they want you to think," Chris said.

"You have a suspicious mind. I like that in a woman." I sipped my drink. My third coffee of the day. No wonder I was getting a buzz. "Do you mind if I ask a few questions?"

"Have at it," she invited. "I'll answer the ones I like and ignore the ones I don't."

That sounded fair enough. Especially considering that I'd lost control of this interview a long time ago.

"How well did you know Lila Moran?"

Chris shrugged. "Not as well as you might think, since we'd worked in the same office for a year. We got along well enough in our professional setting."

"But apparently you weren't friends," I said.

"No, not really."

"Are you friends with the other people you work with?"

Chris nodded. "Most of them, yeah. But Lila was different."

"How?"

"She always seemed to hold herself apart. Lila didn't talk about her family, or her hobbies, or her plans for the weekend. She listened when the rest of us were sharing stuff, but she almost never joined in."

Interesting. That wasn't at all the impression I'd gotten from Karen.

"How did the other people in your office feel about her?" I asked.

"Like maybe you're thinking it was just me she didn't get along with?" Chris grinned. "Nope, that wasn't it. If you asked around, I'd imagine you'd hear that none of us liked her much." She paused, then added, "Except maybe the partners."

"Oh?"

"Well, you know, they're important."

"And you aren't?"

"Not in Lila's eyes, we weren't. The partners were the big shots. She was always going out of her way to try and impress them." Chris pulled a face. "Or if we had a client stop by, Lila would suddenly turn into the sweetest woman you ever met. The rest of us weren't fooled by that act."

She picked up the last piece of lemon cake with her

fingers, tossed it in her mouth, and chewed happily. There went that chance. I hoped it had been good.

"I'll tell you what," Chris said after she'd washed the cake down with a swallow of espresso. "The woman was a hypocrite. The office may be in an uproar now, but after things get back to normal, I won't be the only one who's happy not to have to deal with her crap anymore."

"Karen mentioned a conversation she and Lila had concerning the caretaker on the estate where Lila was living," I said. "She told me you were there too."

"Was I? I don't remember that. All I knew was that she lived in some fancy place in New Canaan."

"Lila needed to have her furnace fixed," I prompted. "And she was afraid of the man who was supposed to come and do it."

"Really? That's odd." Chris looked down at the empty plate and frowned. She seemed more upset that there was no more pound cake than she was about Lila's murder. "Why didn't she just hire another guy?"

"Because the caretaker is responsible for the property," I told her. "It was his job. None of this sounds familiar to you?"

"Nope." She shrugged. "Not one bit. But Lila could be a pretty tough cookie when she didn't get her own way. I can't imagine her being afraid of some repairman."

"That's what Karen told me," I said again.

"Then she must have spent more time chatting with Lila than I did." There was plenty of snark in Chris's tone. "Which is not surprising, considering that her husband, George, is a partner."

It felt like our conversation had come full circle. I started to gather up my things.

When I stood up, Chris remained seated. She didn't

appear to be in any hurry to return to her office. "I do know one thing about Lila you didn't ask about," she said as I was putting on my coat. "She had a boyfriend."

I sank back down in my chair.

"At least she mentioned a guy once. We were talking about how hard it is to meet single men in Fairfield County, and she said she had someone. Mostly, I think, so she could lord it over us that she had a man when the rest of us were still looking. The guy had a really snooty-sounding name. That's why it stuck in my mind. Lincoln Landry."

"You're right." I smiled. "He sounds like a trust fund baby."

"Which probably means he works in a gas station." Chris laughed. "That would serve her right."

"I don't suppose you know how I can get in touch with him?"

"Seriously? Google is your friend. With a name like that, how hard can he be to find?"


"How come we don't have a Christmas tree yet?" Kevin asked that night. "Everyone else has one. How will Santa Claus find us if we don't have a tree?"

It was Kev's bedtime. He'd had a bath and a story, and now he was tucked beneath the covers. Bud was snuggled on the quilt at the foot of his bed. I'd been just about to turn off his light.

And now Kevin wanted to talk. Of course.

"What's that?" Sam came walking around the corner. Faith was lying down in the doorway. She'd been waiting to accompany me back downstairs. Sam stepped over her and entered the room. "You don't think Santa will be able to find you?"

"Not without a tree, and lights, and ornaments," Kevin said plaintively.

"You wrote him a letter, didn't you?" I asked.

Kev nodded.

"And you put your address on it, right?" said Sam.

"I did," Kevin confirmed. "Davey helped. Do you think Santa will read it?"

"I know he will," I told him. "One of the elves will give it to him. Santa Claus reads all the letters children send him."

"He'll see the return address," Sam added. "That's how he'll know where you are."

"Plus, we'll be getting our Christmas tree on Saturday," I said.

Kev brightened briefly. Then he frowned. "That's still two whole days away."

"What's going on? Where is everybody? Is someone having a party in here?" Davey stuck his head in the room. Augie was with him. That big Poodle hopped over Faith too. Then he saw Bud on the bed and jumped up to join him.

At this rate, I was never going to get that child to sleep.

"Kevin thinks we need a Christmas tree," I said.

"Smart kid." Davey and Kevin high-fived. "Of course we need a tree. We're going this weekend."

"We should have one already." Kev pouted. He's single-minded. And stubborn. I have no idea where he gets that from.

"Well, sure," said Davey. "But remember last year, when we went to the Christmas tree farm in Wilton and cut down our own tree? Don't you want to do that again?"

Kevin nodded.

"We can't do it during the week because it takes too long, and by the time I get home from school, it's already starting to get dark. That's why we're going Saturday morning."

Kev considered that for a few seconds. "First thing, right?"

"First thing," the three of us repeated solemnly.

"Promise?"

"We promise," we said.

"Pinky swear?"

"Enough!" I laughed. I got up off the bed and shooed Augie down too. Bud could stay. He always did. "If you don't go to sleep, it will never be Saturday."

"Okay." Kevin closed his eyes. "Turn off the light."

We all snuck out. I closed the door most of the way behind us.

"That kid's crazy for Christmas," Davey said as we all went trooping down the stairs. "Was I that bad at his age?"

"You were worse," I told him.


Claire called later that night. She was whispering into the phone. "Melanie, you have to help me!"

Oh no, I thought. Not again.

I'd been sitting on the couch, reading a book. Faith was lying on the cushion next to me. When I snapped upright, she jumped up too.

"Claire," I said urgently, "where are you?"

"I'm at home. Where do you think? It's almost ten o'clock."

My shoulders relaxed. Okay, so there wasn't any immediate danger. I gave Faith a reassuring pat. She turned a small circle and lay back down.

"What's the matter?" I said.

"I've lost my gold bracelet. The one Bob gave me when we got married. I've looked all over the house and it isn't here. So I thought back to the last time I saw it, and I realized there's only one place it could be."

I squeezed my eyes shut. *Don't say it*, I prayed. *Please don't say it.*

Claire said it. "It's in Lila's cottage."

"No, it's not," I told her firmly. "Think again. I'm sure there are plenty of other places you might have lost it. Besides, weren't you wearing mittens that day?"

"Not when I first went into the gatehouse. I took the mittens off because I knew I'd have to use the key. The bracelet must have slipped off my wrist when I put all those packages down on the table. I remember feeling something tug and I was going to check on it, but then I saw Lila and everything else flew straight out of my mind."

I sighed. Unfortunately that sounded plausible. "If your bracelet was in the gatehouse, the police will have found it by now."

"Maybe," she allowed. "But it could have rolled under a piece of furniture and nobody noticed it. So I have to retrieve it before that detective gets his hands on it and decides it somehow makes me look guilty."

"Claire, that's not going to happen."

"You don't know that," she wailed. Then her voice

dropped to a whisper again. "This is important, Melanie. I need that bracelet back before Bob realizes it's gone."

"I wouldn't worry about that," I said, biting back a smile. After all, the guy was my ex. "Bob isn't that observant."

"He notices more than you think. And I always wear the bracelet, so he's bound to notice that it's not on my wrist. Will you help me?"

"Claire, think for a minute. Even if the police haven't found your bracelet, I know they will have removed the spare key. So how are we going to get inside the gatehouse?"

"Remember that warped window I told you about? It doesn't close all the way, so it can't be locked. I'm sure I can get us in."

I swallowed heavily. This was *so* not a good idea. "Just to clarify, you're proposing that we break into a crime scene?"

"When you put it like that, you make it sound crazy," Claire grumbled.

Frankly, I couldn't think of any other way to put it. Faith was listening to our conversation. Even she looked concerned.

"Yes," she confirmed. "That's what I want to do. And there's nobody else I can ask to come with me. *Please*?"

"When?" I said. I still wasn't making any promises.

"Tomorrow morning. I'll pick you up at seven-thirty, and we can go together. Trust me, we'll be in and out of there in five minutes. Ten, tops."

I did trust Claire. But I still had a sneaking suspicion that things weren't going to go as smoothly as she thought they would.

"We're out in ten minutes," I said. "Whether we've found the bracelet or not."

"I swear," she replied.

I ended the connection and gazed down at Faith. The big Poodle still looked worried. In dog years she was old enough to be my mother. Maybe that was why she'd always felt compelled to watch out for me. Even when I did things she didn't approve of. Perhaps especially then.

"It'll be a quick trip," I told her. "Nobody will even know we were there."

Faith lowered her head and rested her muzzle between her paws. She wasn't convinced of the wisdom of this plan. Sadly, I couldn't blame her.

# Chapter Eight

As it happened, I never got around to mentioning the plan to Sam. I did tell him that he was in charge of getting both boys off to school the next morning. That was cause for a raised eyebrow.

"Claire's picking me up early," I said. "There's something we need to do."

"Do I want to know?"

"Probably not." I smiled to soften the sentiment. I knew it hadn't worked when I heard Sam's next question.

"Do I need to start raising bail money?"

"I hope not," I told him cheerfully.

Sam didn't think that was funny. That put him and Faith on the same team, which wasn't reassuring.

"I hope you know what you're doing," I said to Claire the next morning when I climbed into her car.

We were close to the shortest day of the year and the sun was barely up. The temperature outside was frigid, and there was frost on the grass in my yard. The air smelled like snow. I wondered if that meant some was on the way. I hadn't had time to look at a forecast.

"Of course I don't know what I'm doing," Claire replied. She put the Honda in reverse and backed down the driveway. "That's why I asked you to come along."

That was just peachy.

"Faith thinks we're nuts," I mentioned.

"Faith's a dog. We don't have to take her opinion into account unless we want to." Her gaze swiveled my way. "Which we don't. I'm guessing you didn't tell Sam where you were going?"

"Not exactly," I admitted.

"Good."

Claire turned her eyes back to the road and drove. It wasn't long before we were on Forest Glen Lane. The Mannerly estate loomed into view.

"Oh, look," I said, when we reached the entrance. "There's a gate across the driveway."

"There was a gate there two days ago," Claire replied drily. "Didn't you notice?"

"Two days ago it was open," I pointed out. "Now it's closed. Uh-oh."

"No problem." Claire pulled the car over beside an entry box, discreetly painted black, that I hadn't noticed on my previous visit. "How do you think I got in the other day? Lila gave me the code."

"Of course she did," I muttered under my breath. "That's lucky," I said aloud.

"Or good planning," she informed me.

The double gates swung open. Claire pulled the car

through and they closed behind us. We coasted thirty feet to the gatehouse. The small building looked dark and deserted. The weak morning sun did nothing to brighten its appearance.

A piece of bright yellow crime scene tape was tacked across the cottage's front door. Claire and I both pretended we didn't see it. She pulled around the back and parked in the same spot she'd used the other day.

"Too bad there's no place to hide the car," I said as we got out.

"Hide it from whom?" Claire asked. "Take a look around, Melanie. There's nobody here to see us."

So far, so good.

"Where's the window you were telling me about?"

"It's on the other side."

Claire began to beat her way through the underbrush that had grown up next to the house. Wearing thick boots, flannel-lined jeans, and an oilskin jacket, she was dressed for the job. My clothes were equally heavy, but I was all in black. Earlier that morning, that had struck me as the kind of outfit one ought to wear for housebreaking.

We didn't have to go far. And with Claire breaking a trail in front of me, all I had to do was follow behind. The window looked as though it opened into a storage room next to the kitchen.

As I drew closer, I could see a sliver of an opening between the window frame and the sill. Claire was already trying to wedge her fingers into the small gap. It wasn't working.

"Here," I said. "Let me try."

I started to move forward, but Claire held her place. "No, I have a better idea." She reached into a deep pocket on her jacket and pulled out a crowbar.

I shouldn't have been surprised. Claire was one of the best planners I knew. Of course she would have come prepared.

So instead I just shifted out of the way. "Be careful you don't break the window."

She gave me a withering look. "Really? Lila was always trying to get this place repaired, and nothing ever got fixed. Who's going to notice a little broken glass?"

Claire slipped the claw of the crowbar in beneath the window frame. When she levered the shaft downward, the window rose with a sharp squeal. The size of the chink quickly grew from one inch to six. Then Claire was able to get her hands in place and lift the window the rest of the way. That done, she stepped back.

"You're smaller," she told me. "You go first. If you can't get in through there, there's no hope that I will."

The opening wasn't big, but we were motivated. Three minutes later, we were both inside the gatehouse. It was just as cold inside the building as it was outside. I unzipped my jacket anyway, but I left my gloves on. Claire did the same.

The small room we found ourselves in had probably been a pantry once. Shelves, most of them empty, lined three of the four walls. Two steps took us from there into the kitchen.

I walked over to the table. There was no sign of the presents Claire had left piled there. I wondered where they'd gone.

"This is where you think your bracelet fell off?" I asked.

"Right." Claire was already down on her hands and knees, her gaze scanning the floor. "It has to be here somewhere."

Ten fruitless minutes later, we'd checked every inch of the kitchen. The bracelet was nowhere to be seen. I was ready to concede defeat. And eager for us to be on our way.

"Maybe it rolled into the living room," Claire said.

Our gazes shifted in that direction. Lila's body was long gone, but no one had cleaned the cottage since. Neither of us wanted to step into the next room.

I stood up and dusted off my knees. Claire was about to follow suit when the back door to the gatehouse suddenly flew open. I jumped out of the way just in time. The door bounced off the wall with a loud crash.

Claire screamed and leapt to her feet. She'd put the crowbar down on the kitchen table. I snatched it up and held it out in front of us like a weapon. The move was pure reflex. It wasn't like I was actually going to hit anyone with it.

*Was I?*

A man stood backlit in the open doorway. He was short, broad shouldered, and built like a tree stump. He had his feet braced wide apart and his hands fisted at his sides. A flat cap, pulled low over his forehead, put much of his face in shadow.

"Who the hell are you?" he demanded.

Adrenaline was coursing through me. Otherwise I might have behaved with more moderation. Instead I felt like I wanted to punch someone.

"Who the hell are you?" I shot right back.

"Hank Peebles. I'm the caretaker for this estate. And the two of you are trespassing." He motioned toward the crowbar. "Put that damn thing down before you hurt someone."

"How do I know you are who you say you are?" I asked.

The man grinned. His teeth were stained by tobacco juice. "Because—unlike you two—I have a key to let myself in here. Don't tell me you broke a window with that thing, or you'll be in even more trouble than you already are."

"We didn't have to break in," Claire said, her cheeks flushed. "The window was already open."

"Is that so?" He leaned back against the doorjamb. "And how would you have known that?"

"Because I was friends with the woman who lived here."

"The dead woman," Peebles spat out.

I'd started to lay down the crowbar. Now I lifted it again. Something about this man brought out the worst in me. Probably my suspicion that he'd had a hand in Lila's death.

"Did you kill her?" I asked.

Abruptly he straightened. "What kind of question is that? Of course I didn't kill her. Damn woman must have gotten someone all riled up, but it wasn't me. Is that why you're here? A couple of lookie-loos thinking it might be fun to check out the spot where it happened?"

"No, we came to look for something we lost."

"Oh yeah?" He looked skeptical. "And what would that be?"

"A bracelet," Claire told him. "I dropped it here a couple days ago. Melanie came to help me look for it."

"A bracelet," Peebles repeated with a smirk. "It must be something special to make you break the law for it. You two are trespassers. This is private property—and clearly marked as such. You got no right to be here. Especially not after what happened earlier in the week. I've called the police. They're already on their way."

Claire and I exchanged a look. That wasn't good.

"How did you know we were here?" I asked.

Peebles continued to stand in the open doorway. He was blocking the exit like he thought we might try to escape. It wasn't as if the idea hadn't crossed my mind.

"Not that it's any of your business, but I got a buzzer that lets me know anytime the gate opens," he said. "This is a big estate. I can't be everywhere at once. But I still gotta keep an eye out. Miss Mannerly, she's a very private lady. She doesn't like strangers—people like you—coming around where they don't belong."

He turned to glance outside. Moments later, I heard the sound of an approaching car. A patrol car pulled up beside the gatehouse. Two men got out. The first was a uniformed officer. The second man was Detective Hronis.

*Oh joy.*

Beside me, Claire uttered a small squeak of alarm. Yeah, that was helpful. She was the one whose powers of persuasion had gotten us into this mess. I could only hope that now she'd be persuasive enough to talk our way out.

"Hello, Hank," the officer said as he and the Detective came inside through the open doorway. "What do you have here?"

"These two ladies want me to believe they came here looking for a lost bracelet," Peebles told him. "It sounds fishy to me."

Detective Hronis looked at us. His brow furrowed in a frown. "Ms. Travis," he said. "And Ms. Travis."

"Hello, Detective," I replied.

"You know them?" the officer asked.

"I'm afraid so. I can handle it from here."

Peebles and the officer dropped back. Together they stepped outside.

Hronis looked at me and held out his hand. For a moment, I was confused. Then I realized what he wanted. I handed over the crowbar.

"Any other weapons in your possession?" he asked.

Claire and I shook our heads.

"I'm guessing you didn't see the crime scene tape on the door?"

"We did," said Claire. "That's why we came in through the window."

"The window," he repeated.

"In the pantry," I told him. "It's warped."

He blinked, tipped his head to one side. "And that made it seem like a good idea for you to come back here and check things out? You realize this is a crime scene, right? There's a reason why it's secure."

The detective's gaze shifted to Claire. "So you were looking for something you left behind. Maybe some kind of evidence you didn't want me to find? Is that why we're all standing here in the cold?"

"No." Her voice squeaked. "That's not it at all."

I loved Claire, but she was a terrible liar. And the glare she sent my way clearly said, "I told you so!"

"Well, then." Hronis crossed his arms over his chest. "The two of you had better tell me what's going on before I decide to take you both down to the station to continue this conversation."

"That won't be necessary," I said quickly.

"I hope not. But so far, you haven't given me any reason to think differently."

"It's all my fault," Claire blurted. "Melanie had nothing to do with it."

She told him about the lost bracelet, given to her by her husband on their wedding day. She explained how it must have fallen off when she put down the parcels. She insisted that all we'd meant to do was retrieve it, then quickly leave.

"*After* you'd contaminated my crime scene," Hronis said.

Claire held up her hands. "We wore gloves."

He growled under his breath. "So I guess it didn't occur to you to call me and ask if we'd found it? Or if someone from the department could escort you over here to have a look?"

"Ummm," Claire said slowly. "No."

"Any particular reason why not?"

"Because I thought you'd say no," Claire admitted.

"You're not helping your case any, Ms. Travis," Hronis said forcefully. "I would have said no. Because you have no business being here. You're lucky I believe your story, cockeyed as it is, because otherwise I'd have to arrest you. And that would lead to a lot of unnecessary paperwork for everybody."

I hadn't realized until that moment that I'd been holding my breath. Now I exhaled slowly. A small puff of condensation blew out into the cold air.

"Thank you for believing us," I said.

Hronis shot me an aggrieved look. "I don't want your thanks. I just want you to stay out of my hair."

"We'll certainly try," I said with feeling.

"See that you do."

We followed him outside. He pulled the door shut behind us. I was ready to go. But now that the detective had released us, Claire chose that moment to decide to be helpful.

"I know something," she piped up.

"Is that so?" Hronis turned in her direction. He propped his hands on his hips. "Let's hear it."

"Lila Moran wasn't her real name."

The detective's expression didn't change. He still looked exasperated. "And you know that, how?"

"Because before I took her on as a client, I looked into her background." When his eyes narrowed, Claire quickly added, "I do it with all my clients. And I couldn't find any information about Lila that was more than five years old. It was as if she didn't exist before that."

The caretaker and the police officer had been standing off to one side, talking to each other. But now I saw Peebles abruptly fall silent. He appeared to be listening to what Claire had to say.

"Thank you, Ms. Travis," Hronis replied. "We are aware of that."

Claire smiled brightly, like a student trying to please a difficult teacher. "That could be a clue, right?"

"Maybe." His tone was noncommittal. "It would have been more helpful if you'd told me earlier. Before we'd already found out for ourselves. And speaking of things we found out, here's something else I know. You two ladies aren't sisters."

*Oops.*

I stopped staring at the caretaker and turned my attention back to the conversation in front of me. It seemed it had suddenly become more critical to my well-being than whatever Hank Peebles was up to.

"Claire and I aren't actual sisters," I told the detective. "But we're as close as sisters."

"That isn't what you told Officer Jenkins."

"Maybe he misunderstood," I said.

"He didn't." The detective frowned. Again. "Let me tell you something, Ms. Travis. Lying to the police is a dumb thing to do. Especially when we're investigating a murder."

"You're right," I agreed. "Absolutely."

"So bearing that in mind, is there anything else you might want to tell me?"

"Actually, there is." I lowered my voice. "But maybe not right here."

Detective Hronis wasn't stupid. He immediately caught on to what I meant. He cupped a hand around my upper arm and led me around to the other side of the gatehouse. When he was satisfied that he'd put enough distance between us and the others, he stopped and said, "What?"

"Hank Peebles, the guy who takes care of this property—I guess you know him?"

"We've met before today."

"Lila Moran was afraid of him."

"How do you know that?"

"She told a woman named Karen Clauson that Peebles was supposed to be making repairs on the cottage, but she was scared to let him inside. Lila thought he meant to take something from her."

"You have any idea what that item might have been?"

I shook my head.

"Clauson," the detective said. "Bit of an unusual name. Is she related to George Clauson, who worked with Ms. Moran at James and Brant?"

"Karen is his wife," I told him.

"I guess that means we'll have to have a chat with her." Hronis started to return to the others. Then he stopped and turned back. "Once I found out that you two weren't really sisters, I asked around about you."

He paused, waiting for me to comment. So help me, I couldn't think of a single useful thing to say.

"I heard you are the kind of person who likes to get herself involved in police business."

I cleared my throat softly. My gaze skittered away from his. "That might occasionally be true."

"I also heard you're the kind of person who sometimes comes up with good ideas."

I looked back at him. That sounded more promising.

"So let me tell you how this is going to work," he said. "I think you should keep your nose to yourself. But if you should happen to find out something that pertains to this case, you bring it straight to me. Understand?"

And just like that, I felt chastised again.

"Yes, sir," I replied.

Hronis stopped just short of rolling his eyes.

"What was that private conversation about?" Claire asked when we were back in the car, making our escape.

"Mostly Detective Hronis wanted to warn me to stop asking questions."

"Yeah, right." Claire smirked and kept driving. "Like that's going to work."

# Chapter
# Nine

I was back home by 10:00 a.m. Sam wasn't there when Claire dropped me off, which was a relief. I had no desire to rehash the morning's ill-advised adventure in the conversation I knew would inevitably follow. At least Sam hadn't had to come up with bail money.

I'd already taken Chris Sanchez's advice and done an internet search for Lincoln Landry. It turned out she'd been mostly right about a couple of things. First, he wasn't hard to find. And second, Landry didn't work in a gas station, but close. He was a car mechanic.

I popped into the house and took the Poodle pack out for a quick play session in the backyard. Then, with apologies all around, I left the dogs again and drove back to New Canaan.

Fred's Fine Motor Repair was located on a side street

near the downtown area. The business was housed in a squat brick building that was older than I was. A parking lot out front was littered with vehicles in various states of repair. Most appeared to be of foreign origin: BMWs and Mercedes rather than Toyotas and Mazdas. The garage next to the office had just two bays, but there were cars up on both lifts. Even so, there didn't seem to be much activity going on.

The office had a glass door. A buzzer sounded loudly enough to make me jump when I pushed it open. The small room must have also served as a waiting area because there were several tattered chairs pushed against one wall. A table between them held a stack of magazines that had been current the previous summer.

"Be right with you!" someone called from the garage.

Two minutes later, a door behind the counter swung open. A man wearing a jumpsuit with the name FRED stenciled on the pocket came inside. He was busy wiping his hands on a dirty rag, which gave me a few moments to study him.

He had dark, curly hair and the kind of chiseled features more likely to be seen on a fashion runway than sliding out from beneath a car. Even in the baggy jumpsuit, his body looked impressive. When I glanced up again, I was startled to find myself locking gazes with a pair of piercing brown eyes. The man had been assessing me with the same intensity with which I'd focused on him.

Now he favored me with a slow, sure, grin. We'd just met, and I already knew that the man was a player. And obviously he knew I'd liked what I'd seen. *Dammit.*

"Hello," I said. "I'm looking for Lincoln Landry."

"That's me."

I wasn't sure whether or not to believe him. Maybe he

thought we were flirting, making a connection. If so, I was ready to shut him down.

I pointed toward his pocket. "Your name tag says Fred."

"That's right." He was still grinning.

"But that's not your name?"

"Fred's the owner. He hasn't worked in the garage for more than a decade. But customers don't know that. Fred, the owner, says that people like to deal with the man in charge. So we all wear name tags that say FRED on them. That way everybody's happy."

"Except maybe me," I muttered. "So you're really Lincoln Landry?"

"Linc, please. No one calls me by my full name except my mother." He extended a hand over the counter so we could shake. "And you are?"

"Melanie Travis."

"Well, Melanie Travis, what can I do for you? I see your Volvo out there. If you're having problems with it, you've come to the right place. Foreign cars are our specialty."

"No, my car is fine," I said. "I was hoping I could ask you a few questions about a friend of yours. Lila Moran?"

Linc screwed up his face in concentration. "Who?"

"Lila Moran," I tried again. "She worked at James and Brant in Stamford?"

He still looked blank.

*Now what*? I wondered. I'd never met Lila, so it wasn't as though I could describe her. Was it possible that Linc had so many girlfriends, he couldn't keep them all straight?

"She lived here in New Canaan on the Mannerly estate?"

Finally I saw a glimmer of recognition. "Oh. You mean Lily Mo."

Lila Moran . . . Lily Mo? I supposed that was close enough.

"Sure," I said. "Lily Mo. When was the last time you saw her?"

He thought back. "Maybe three, four, days ago when she dropped off her car." He pointed to a silver Kia that was sitting outside in the lot. "She's due back anytime to pick it up."

"She's due back . . . ?" I repeated slowly. Was it possible he didn't know? "Lila isn't coming back to get her car. I'm very sorry to have to tell you that she was killed in her home at the beginning of the week."

"Killed?" Linc sounded as though he didn't understand the word. "Like, she's dead?"

"Yes. I'm so sorry for your loss. I thought you would have already heard the news. The police are investigating what happened."

"My loss?" Linc shook his head, as if he was still having a hard time processing what I'd told him. "Wait a minute. What are you talking about?"

"Lila told her friends that you and she were a couple," I said. "Wasn't she your girlfriend?"

"No." It was the first definite thing he'd said since the conversation began. "No, Lily was *not* my girlfriend. She told you that?"

"She told several people," I confirmed.

"And now she's dead?"

"I'm afraid so."

He sagged back against the wall behind him. "I can hardly believe it."

"If Lila wasn't your girlfriend, what was the nature of your relationship?" I asked.

"I wouldn't call it a relationship." Abruptly Linc straightened. "Lily and I met at a bar a couple of months ago. We had a few drinks, spent a little time together . . ."

"How much time?"

"Two weeks, no more than that. She lived in an odd little house behind a big gate. The place was in the middle of a forest. And it was falling down around her ears. Going there gave me the willies. It was like visiting the witch's cottage in a Grimms' fairy tale."

"Is that why you stopped seeing her?" I was guessing that he'd been the one to end the relationship—or if he hadn't, he'd still remember it that way.

"Nah, that wasn't it. Lily was just too intense for me. Everything was guarded with her. She never said a single word without thinking about it first. Me, I'm more of a free spirit. I like to take things as they come. Life's too short to sweat the small stuff. And that wasn't her style at all."

"Was there anything inside the cottage—one of her possessions maybe—that Lila seemed particularly concerned about?"

"Not that I can think of." Linc was back to looking baffled. "Why?"

"I was wondering whether the person who killed her might have been looking for something."

"I wouldn't know about that." He stopped and frowned. Something had occurred to him. Linc didn't appear to be the brightest bulb. I figured I'd better grab the thought before he lost it again.

"What?" I asked.

"A couple times when I was with Lily, she got these

phone calls. She'd look down at the number, drop whatever she was doing, and say, 'I have to take this.' Then she'd go into another room and shut the door. Like she wanted to make sure that I didn't hear what she was saying."

"Did you ask her about it?"

"No way. Why would I want to do that? It's not as if she was my *girlfriend* or anything. If Lily wanted to keep secrets, it was none of my business. Just like what I was up to on the side was none of hers. Plenty of fish in the sea, you know what I mean?"

Linc winked at me then. He actually winked. Was there a woman in the world who would find that juxtaposition endearing? I sincerely hoped not.

"Detective Hronis is the man in charge of the investigation into Lila's death," I said. "If you think of anything else, you should give him a call."

Maybe that would earn me some brownie points with the police, I thought.

"That's not going to happen," Linc told me. "But if you want to give me your number, I'll call you instead."

There I was, stuck between a rock and a hard place. On one hand, I had no desire to give Linc my phone number. On the other, he might realize after I'd gone that he actually did know something useful.

Before I could think too much about the wisdom of the impulse, I scribbled the number down on a piece of paper and pushed it across the counter. Linc looked at it, then slipped it into his grimy pocket.

"You'll be hearing from me, Melanie Travis," he called after me as I let myself out.

\* \* \*

I left New Canaan and drove straight to Graceland Nursery School to pick up Kevin. He wiggled back and forth as I was buckling him in his car seat.

"Where are we going now?" he asked. "Time to get a Christmas tree?"

I walked around the Volvo and slid into the driver's seat. "No, that's tomorrow."

"That's what you said yesterday." He pouted.

"No, that's what *you* said yesterday."

"I'm confused," Kev told me.

"So am I," I admitted. But it wasn't just Christmas that had my head spinning. For me, it was more of a cosmic "I have no idea what to do next" kind of thing.

I glanced back at him over my shoulder. "But you know who's a good person to talk to when you're confused?"

"Santa Claus?" Kev squealed happily.

"No. Aunt Peg."

"Oh." He slumped in his seat.

"She has puppies," I reminded him. "I bet she'll let you play with them."

He perked up a bit at that. "Puppies with funny names. Are they Poodles?"

"No, these three look like Australian Shepherds."

"Shepherds." Kevin turned the word over in his mind. "There were shepherds in the manger when Jesus was born."

I thought about explaining the difference. I truly did. But there was traffic on the Merritt Parkway, and I needed to keep my eyes on the road. So instead I said, "These will be just the same."

"Cool beans," Kev replied.

I'd called ahead, and Aunt Peg was expecting us. In

fact, the front door to her house was open before we were even halfway down the driveway. There was an enormous pine cone- and cranberry-covered wreath on her door, but I noted that she had yet to rehang the Christmas stocking that had been on her mailbox.

Five Standard Poodles came spilling down the outside steps to greet us. Once I'd gotten Kevin out of the car, we took a minute to return their enthusiastic greeting. Still, it hardly took us any time to reach the house.

That wasn't fast enough for Aunt Peg, who was radiating impatience. She stood in the doorway with her arms crossed over her chest and her sneaker-clad foot tapping on the threshold. When we all reached the porch, Aunt Peg quickly ushered the Poodles inside the house, then turned to confront me.

"So," she said with relish, "I hear you almost got yourself arrested this morning."

"Shush!" I looked around for Kevin. Luckily, he'd followed the Poodles down the hallway. It looked as though the gang was heading toward the kitchen, where the puppies were stashed. "If you tell Kevin, he'll tell Sam."

"Meaning you don't intend to?"

"I'll own up to it eventually," I said, shrugging out of my coat. "I just want to make sure the incident has the right spin when he hears about it. Let's get Kev settled with the puppies. Then we can talk."

Kevin had shed his outerwear as he'd trotted down the hallway. I followed behind and gathered everything up. When Aunt Peg and I reached the kitchen, my son was pressed against the baby gate that barred the doorway.

"How come they can't come out?" he asked.

"They're just babies, so it's safer to keep them confined," Aunt Peg told him. "But we can go in." She slipped her hands beneath his armpits and hoisted him over the waist-high gate. "Now sit down on the floor and give them a call."

The blue puppy was curled up, asleep, on a sheepskin mat. The two black males were wrestling over a stuffed toy. But when Kevin clapped his hands, all three fuzzy puppies came galloping across the floor.

The trio had grown and changed, even in the two days since I'd last seen them. The puppies were steadier on their feet now, and they liked to hear themselves bark. Their tiny ears flapped up and down as they ran. Kev giggled with delight as all three Aussies tried to climb up in his lap at the same time.

"Enjoy yourself," Aunt Peg told him. "Your mother and I are going to chat for a few minutes. While we're doing that, see if you can guess which name goes with which puppy."

She poured me a cup of instant coffee. Usually, I have to make my own, so I took that as a sign of her eagerness for updates. There was a plate of brownies on the counter, along with a mug of Earl Grey tea. Busy with the puppies, Kevin didn't even notice the sweets. I figured that meant we could speak with privacy.

I grabbed my coffee and the brownies and sat down at the kitchen table. Aunt Peg brought her tea and joined me.

"You've been talking to Claire," I said, nabbing a brownie from the plate between us.

"Of course I've been talking to Claire," she replied. "Somebody has to keep me apprised of what's going on. It sounds as though the two of you had quite an adventure."

"Not on purpose. The plan was to slip in and out before anyone noticed we were there."

"You can't seriously have believed that would be possible." The snort that accompanied that statement was rather rude. "Josie Mannerly is a famous recluse, with enough money to ensure that people have to respect her wish for privacy. If anyone could come and go from that estate on a whim, the tabloids would be all over her. Especially now, after what happened there."

"You're right." I sighed. "It was an ill-conceived idea from the start. But Claire was determined and I didn't want her to go by herself."

"So she told me. She seemed to think that you should be absolved of blame. I'm withholding judgment myself." Aunt Peg paused for a large bite of her brownie. "Tell me everything. Start with the caretaker who waylaid you."

Despite her request, I couldn't start there. If I wanted the narrative to make sense, I had to backtrack. Aunt Peg had spoken with Claire about the morning's events, but she didn't know about the conversations I'd had the day before with Karen Clauson and Chris Sanchez. So I summarized those first. Then I jumped ahead to our encounter with Hank Peebles.

"I can understand why Lila was afraid of him," I said. "I know he scared the crap out of me."

"Do you suppose Karen Clauson was correct and there's something he wants inside that gatehouse?"

"Maybe." I stopped and frowned. "But apparently, he has a key to the place. So if he wanted to conduct a search, what would prevent him from entering anytime he wished?"

"Maybe the object he's after is new," Aunt Peg mused. "Or maybe he just found out about it. Perhaps he used the key to let himself inside the cottage the other day, not realizing that Lila was home at the time."

I nodded slowly. "You could be onto something. Because Lila's car was in the shop for repairs. So Peebles could have seen that it was gone, and figured he had free access to do whatever he wanted."

"Thereby precipitating the confrontation that led to her death," Aunt Peg said triumphantly.

I picked at my brownie. Chewy and oozing with chocolate, it tasted homemade, even though I knew it came from a bakery downtown.

"Except that Lila was shot," I pointed out. "If Peebles thought the cottage was empty, why would he have brought a gun with him?"

"Maybe that was Lila's gun." Aunt Peg played devil's advocate. "Maybe she accosted him, and he disarmed her. Have the police found the weapon that was used to kill her?"

I rolled my eyes until she got the message.

"You mean to tell me that even after your friendly chat this morning, Detective Hronis isn't keeping you informed of new developments?"

"I wouldn't exactly characterize our talk as friendly," I told her. "It was more like the good detective was advising me to stay out of his way."

"Oh pish. That's what the authorities always say. You know they don't mean it."

Earlier in the year, Aunt Peg had struck up a friendship with a detective from the Stamford Police Department. It had been the highlight of her summer. The two of them had become so chummy that she'd even added Detective Sturgill to her Christmas card list.

I didn't seem to have the same kind of luck with the police.

"They do mean it," I said.

She gave me a knowing smile. "Then it's a good thing you've never been particularly adept at following directions."

# Chapter
# Ten

"Hey!" Kevin suddenly looked up at us. "Nobody told me there were brownies."

"You didn't ask, you silly boy. Of course there are brownies," Aunt Peg said. "But if you want one, you have to come and join us at the table."

Kev's gaze dropped. Both male puppies were asleep in his lap. The blue girl was chewing on the tip of his shoe. He was clearly undecided. She'd given him a tough choice. "But the puppies are down here."

"It's a dilemma, isn't it?" she agreed. "Why don't you stay there and I'll pack a brownie for you to take with you when you leave?"

"Yes, please."

I was marveling at my son's polite answer when one of the black boys lifted his head and nipped at Kevin's finger. He giggled and pulled his hand away. Then he reached back and scratched under the puppy's chin. In the space of seconds, Kev had forgotten all about us.

"More for me," Aunt Peg said happily. She slid another brownie onto her napkin. "Now go on. Surely that can't be all you've accomplished since the last time we saw each other."

"It isn't. I also had a chat this morning with Lila's supposed boyfriend."

"Supposed?" She glanced up. "What does that mean?"

"It means that he didn't think he was in a relationship with her. Linc Landry admitted to knowing Lila but said they'd just had a quick fling."

"He would say that, wouldn't he? The woman is dead. If he has something to hide, it only makes sense that he would want to disassociate himself from her."

"Linc was already having trouble remembering who she was before I told him that she'd been killed," I told her.

Aunt Peg looked surprised. "You mean he didn't know?"

"Apparently not."

"That's ridiculous. New Canaan is a small town. A murder there would be big news. I think your Mr. Landry was lying to you. Maybe he killed Lila, and this was his way of deflecting attention away from himself."

"He did say something else that was interesting."

"It's about time," Aunt Peg muttered under her breath.

I ignored that and pressed on. "Sometimes when they were together, Lila would get phone calls that were important enough for her to immediately stop what she was doing and go in another room to talk."

"Maybe she had a lover," Aunt Peg mused.

"She did," I pointed out. "Linc. And he was standing right there. Maybe she was talking to Josephine Mannerly. Do you think that's a possibility?"

The idea made her smile. "All I know is that if Josie were to call me out of the blue, I would drop everything to talk to her too."

"Josie was Lila's landlady," I said. "Maybe they had stuff to discuss."

"Like overdue rent?" Aunt Peg was skeptical.

"I was thinking more like why that creepy Hank Peebles was always hanging around the gatehouse." I grabbed a second brownie. Or possibly a third. It was hard to talk and keep count at the same time. "Or maybe the mystery caller was someone from Lila's dubious past."

"Ah, yes." Aunt Peg nodded. "Claire finally got around to mentioning that to me. That was quite a tantalizing tidbit for her to keep tucked away, don't you think?"

"I gather she felt we would think less of her if we knew she'd taken on a client with a questionable history."

"Less than if she took on a client who got herself killed?" She lifted a brow. "That's hard to credit."

"I'm ready for my brownie now," Kevin announced. The puppies had gone to sleep on the sheepskin bed. All three had cuddled together to form a small mound. "Is it time to go?"

"Just about," I told him.

"Not so fast." Aunt Peg pushed back her chair and stood. "You were going to guess the puppies' names, remember?"

"I know their names." Kev sounded very pleased with himself. "They're Black, Blue, and Ditto."

"Yes, but which is which? That's the hard part."

"Blue is the blue puppy," Kev told her. "Black is

whichever one of the others comes over first. Then the last one is Ditto."

"That makes perfect sense to me," I said with a laugh.

Aunt Peg couldn't disagree. As she held out her hand, she looked like she wanted to laugh too. "Here, young man. You've earned yourself a brownie."

Saturday morning arrived faster than I'd anticipated. That probably had something to do with the fact that Kevin was out of bed and dressed before I even had my eyes open. And once he was up, that meant all the creatures in the house would be stirring too. As well as my husband and our older son. Everybody couldn't wait to go tramping around a forest on a cold winter day.

I was steaming in a hot shower when Sam opened the bathroom door. "Breakfast is on the table," he said.

I took that as my cue to turn off the stream of water. "What are we having?"

"Cereal. Lots of cereal. More cereal that you can imagine."

I peeked out from behind the shower curtain. Sam tossed me a towel. There was only one thing I could say next. "What did Kevin do now?"

"He decided to hurry us along by feeding the dogs himself. He also decided they must be tired of eating kibble. So he made them eight bowls of cereal. I got to the kitchen just in time to keep him from handing them out."

"Eight?" I wrapped the towel around me and stepped out of the shower. "Kev knows we only have six dogs."

Sam bit back a grin. "He thought Bud looked hungry, so he made him extra servings."

That little mutt was already shaped like a football. He

needed fewer helpings, not additional ones. But Bud was a master at manipulation.

"Bud always looks hungry," I said.

"Kev and I had that conversation," Sam told me. "And we gave the dogs their kibble. Now all we have to do is eat eight bowls of cereal."

"And chop down a Christmas tree," I mentioned.

"Right," said Sam. "That's the fun part. Hurry up."

As he disappeared, I stared after him with a smile on my face. Was there a man in the world who didn't flex his muscles, suck in his gut, and grin with glee when he was handed a chain saw? If so, I wasn't married to him.

Haney's Holiday Home was a Christmas tree farm in northwest Wilton. Situated on ten acres of wooded land, it had been a popular holiday destination for decades, until its elderly owner died and the place was allowed to fall into disrepair. My brother, Frank, and my ex-husband, Bob, who also co-owned a bistro in Stamford, had purchased the property the previous December.

Then it had been a scramble to get the business up and running in time for Christmas. All able-bodied family members had found themselves pressed into service—either to help make repairs or serve as salespeople. This year Frank had been able to plan ahead and he'd hired college students to fill in for the season. After that, all Frank and Bob had had to do was open their doors and customers had come flooding back.

Sam parked his SUV in front of the clapboard office building. I hadn't been back to the tree farm in nearly a year. I could see that there had been additional improvements made in the meantime.

The outside of the structure was freshly painted and the parking lot had been resurfaced. A spruce wreath decorated with silver bells and sprigs of holly was hanging on the office door. Red and white ribbons were twined in a candy cane pattern around the banister that led to the porch. The place looked festive and inviting, and Kevin was already running on ahead to dash up the steps.

"I miss the snow." Davey came over and stood next to me. "Last year when we were here, the snow was up to my knees."

Last year we'd found a dead body half buried in the snow, I thought. I didn't miss anything about that.

"Snow's on the way," said Sam. "It won't be long now. We'll have six inches on the ground before Christmas."

Kev heard that. He'd been reaching for the doorknob, but now he spun around. "Promise?"

"Uh-oh," I said under my breath.

"Promise," Sam agreed.

I punched him in the arm. "What are you going to do if you're wrong?"

"That's easy." He followed his son up the steps. "I'll just blame the weather on you."

It took us half the morning to find the perfect Christmas tree. The cultivated forest around us had plenty of good options. But Davey and Kevin both wanted to have the deciding vote on which tree we brought home, and the two boys couldn't agree on which one to choose.

While they argued over the merits of height versus symmetry of branches, I just stood in the middle of the woods and inhaled deeply. All I wanted was a Christmas tree that smelled great. Fortunately, that part was easy.

It took another hour to cut the tall Douglas fir down, then get it back to the SUV. If the boys hadn't been helping, Sam and I probably could have accomplished those tasks in half the time. Not that it mattered. We had the rest of the day to get the tree up and decorated. It felt great just to kick back and enjoy family time for a change.

When we arrived home, the dogs met us at the door. It wasn't every day we brought a tree inside the house, and apparently, that was cause for canine mayhem.

"I know you remember this," I told Faith. The oldest and the wisest of the Poodles, she was the first to calm down. Tar, Augie, and Bud were still leaping and yapping and otherwise making fools of themselves. "Tell them everything is all right. This is only temporary."

Faith gave me a reproachful look. Just because she remembered didn't mean she thought a tree belonged in her living room.

While Sam and the boys got the Christmas tree set up in its stand, I put on holiday music and poured eggnog for everybody. I added a little kick to Sam's and mine.

That was a good thing, because when I returned to the living room the Poodles were adding to the party by zooming around the room. They bounced from couch to chairs, then back to the floor before racing circles around the tree. Kevin was giggling uncontrollably. He was also slipping Bud and Tar slivers of candy cane when he thought no one was looking.

I started unpacking the ornaments. Sam and Davey untangled the lights and strung them around the tree. Kevin was in charge of tinsel. The boys had chosen a towering Douglas fir, so it took us a while to decorate every inch. Finally everything was in place.

We all stood back to admire the effect.

"Wow," said Kevin.

Davey reached over to ruffle his brother's hair. "Now

Santa Claus will know just where to find you. This tree is so big, I bet it's already on his radar."

Kev turned to him with wide eyes. "Do you think so?"

I didn't hear Davey's answer, because my cell phone began to ring. I'd left it in my bedroom earlier, so I had to make a mad dash for the stairs. Faith came racing behind me. She loved to talk on the phone, especially if Aunt Peg was calling.

I was slightly winded by the time I snatched the phone off the dresser and sank down on the bed. Faith jumped up beside me. I glanced at the screen, then held the device to my ear. Once again, it was Claire.

"You cost me a client," she said without preamble.

"Hi, Claire. Wait . . . *what*?" Abruptly my good mood vanished. "What did you say?"

"You cost me a client," she repeated slowly. "Karen Clauson. I just got off the phone with her. She's furious."

I reached over and pulled Faith into my lap. Dogs are a surefire stress reliever when things go wrong. And suddenly it sounded as though something had gone very wrong. I tangled my fingers in the Poodle's long ear hair.

"Claire, start at the beginning, please. Tell me what happened."

"I set it up so that you and Karen could meet."

"Yes, you did," I agreed. "And she and I had a perfectly pleasant conversation. She didn't seem unhappy when I left."

"Apparently, that was before she realized you were going to go running to the police with the information she gave you."

"Oh," I said. "Right."

In the spirit of sharing—and to take the sting out of the

fact that Claire and I had just been discovered somewhere we definitely didn't belong—I'd related to Detective Hronis what Karen had said about the Mannerly estate caretaker. I'd given him Karen's name. I'd even confirmed that she was George Clauson's wife.

But wait a minute, I thought. What was wrong with that?

"That detective you talked to stopped by her house," said Claire. "This morning, on a Saturday. George was there. And her kids. And apparently a couple of the kids' friends. When a policeman parked right out front and marched into her house as if she'd done something wrong."

"But she hadn't done anything wrong," I sputtered. "He just needed to talk to her. He probably wanted to confirm what I'd told him."

"Yeah, well, I guess that wasn't how it looked to the neighbors. Then George got upset because he hadn't known Karen had previously talked to the police . . . and was she hiding things from him? And her kids got upset when they heard that someone their parents knew had been murdered." Claire stopped and sighed. "You can probably imagine how things snowballed from there."

"It was all a misunderstanding," I said. "Lots of people talk to the police about stuff, and nobody gets upset about it."

"No, Melanie, lots of people do not get involved with the police," Claire said firmly. "*You do*. And the rest of us probably would get upset about it, except that by now you've done it so many times that we just figure, 'What's the point?'"

I bit my lip between my teeth. My eyes blinked rapidly. Suddenly it felt as though I'd been punched in the gut. That wasn't fair. Claire was the one who'd called me when she found Lila. She had asked me to become involved.

Faith sensed my change in mood. She snuggled her warm body closer to mine and laid her head down across my legs. But right now, even she couldn't make me feel better.

"So even though Karen was one of my oldest and best clients," Claire continued, "she has now severed her relationship with me."

"She can't do that," I said hotly.

"Of course she can. Karen is free to take her party planning business anywhere she wants to."

"She's the one who introduced you to Lila Moran. If it wasn't for Karen, you and I wouldn't even be mixed up in this."

"Good point." Claire sounded resigned. "And yet, I'm still fired."

"You can't be fired," I said. "It's not right. I'm going to fix this."

"Don't you dare call Karen. It will only make things worse."

"How can they be worse? You already lost her business. I won't call. I'll go see Karen in person. We'll have another friendly conversation. I'll remind her about all the great parties you've thrown for her. I'll tell her none of this is your fault. Don't worry, I'll get things smoothed over. You'll see."

She hung up without answering.

# Chapter
# Eleven

Okay, so maybe I had an ulterior motive.

Of course I wanted to help Claire win back Karen's account. I hated being the cause of her lost business. But I also hadn't forgotten that Karen had promised to ask her husband about Lila Moran's résumé and the information about her past it might contain. Maybe I was being wildly optimistic, but this seemed like an opportunity to kill two birds with one stone.

Or then again, maybe not.

Karen wasn't amused when I texted her. Her reply came back quickly. **Don't contact me again.**

Fat chance of that, I thought. We needed to talk.

So that's what I told her. And that I was sorry for what had happened. I offered to come by and apologize in person.

Karen shot that idea down in a hurry.

**Please just let me explain**, I texted back.

Faith and I stared at the phone for two full minutes, waiting for a reply. Finally it chirped in my hand.

**Not here. Meet me at West Beach in twenty minutes.**

I picked Faith up and set her aside on the bed. "Sorry," I told the big Poodle. "I have to go."

West Beach was at the upper edge of the Shippan Point peninsula. On a Saturday before Christmas, it would take me at least twenty minutes just to drive there, which meant I was already in a hurry. Plus, it was a beach. So I definitely needed some warm clothing.

I explained to Sam where I was going while I pulled on boots and a coat in the front hall. I promised to be back soon. I stuffed some gloves in my pocket. Sam plopped a hat on my head and told me he'd entertain the kids with bloodthirsty video games while I was gone. I was pretty sure he was kidding about that.

Not surprisingly for a late afternoon in December, the beach at the park was nearly deserted. Long Island Sound looked gray and choppy. The sky above it was opaque. It wasn't hard to find Karen. She was sitting on a slatted bench, waiting for me.

Karen was bundled up against the weather, just like I was. Her puffy down coat covered her from neck to lower thigh, and her blond hair was tucked into a faux fur hat that was pulled low over her ears. Her hands were jammed in her pockets. She stood up as I approached.

"I'll give you five minutes," she said, heading across the sand to the water's edge. "Let's walk."

This close to the winter solstice, the sun went down

early in Connecticut. Dusk was almost already upon us. My feet sank into the deep sand as I hurried to catch up. Karen had made it clear she wasn't going to wait.

"I'm sorry about what happened," I began. "I didn't realize you'd told me those things in confidence."

Not that that would have made a difference, I thought. But still.

Karen gave me a withering look. "George already talked to the detective at his office. It never occurred to me that the man would show up *at my house*, wanting to involve me in his investigation too."

"I'm sorry," I said again. I planned to keep repeating that until she accepted my apology. "But the important thing is that none of this is Claire's fault. If a mistake was made, I'm the one who made it. You shouldn't punish her for something I did."

"Claire isn't one of my children," Karen snapped. "She isn't being *punished*. She's simply having to learn that when you behave badly, your decisions have consequences."

"But that's the point. Claire did nothing wrong."

We'd reached the water. Froth-tipped waves were lapping against the shore. The sand was firmer here, and Karen followed a receding wave out. When a new ripple of water approached, she kicked a spray into the air.

"Claire asked me to talk to you," she said, without turning around. "She should have warned me that it might be a problem. Now George is furious, and that means I'm the one who will have to make amends. It was bad enough that the woman who died was employed by his firm. But to have the scandal intrude upon his personal life, too, is truly beyond the pale."

"I understand that you're upset." Karen continued to

stare out over the Sound, so I was talking to her back. "But a crime was committed. And the police need to solve it. The fact that Lila worked for James and Brant means that your husband was already peripherally involved in their investigation."

Karen still said nothing, so I kept talking. "When we spoke before, you said you'd look into Lila Moran's résumé. What did you find out?"

Her head whipped around. "Why should I do anything to help you now?"

I shrugged. There wasn't anything I could say to convince her. She would either decide to help me or not.

Karen's shoulders were stiff. Her posture radiated annoyance. As she turned to head back across the beach to the parking lot, she said, "There was virtually nothing on Lila's résumé. So I guess the joke's on you. There were only a few current items that didn't even fill up the page."

"That doesn't make sense," I said.

Now it was Karen's turn to shrug. It made no difference to her whether I found her answer satisfactory or not.

We'd almost reached the sidewalk. The parking lot was just beyond. I was running out of time. "How did Lila get a good job at James and Brant without a decent résumé?"

Abruptly Karen stopped. "How would I know that?"

"Because I'm guessing you asked. You're probably as curious as I am."

"Someone pulled strings," she replied shortly. "A big client asked Mr. Brant to hire her, and he did. That's all I know. Are we finished?"

"Almost."

Karen tossed her head. *"What?"*

"Once you get over being angry, you're going to remember that Claire is the best event planner in Fairfield County. And a great way to make amends would be to throw your husband the best party ever. Think about it."

"You gave me a splendid idea the other day," Aunt Peg told me the next morning. She and I were sitting on the ground in her backyard, watching the three Aussie puppies tumble around in the grass. Yes, I know it was December. Coming outside hadn't been my decision.

"Much better footing for puppies than that slippery kitchen floor," Aunt Peg had told me. So out we'd gone.

She and I were supposed to be having a super secret conversation about family Christmas presents. At least that was the pretext under which she'd invited me over. But I'd spent the past ten minutes telling her about my meeting with Karen. And since I couldn't remember any ideas I'd had recently—splendid or otherwise—that would help with Christmas shopping, I suspected the subject was about to be changed again.

I was chilly sitting on the hard ground, but the three wavy-coated puppies were loving the freedom to explore the enclosed yard. They were blossoming under Aunt Peg's care, growing bigger, brighter, and more adventuresome every day. Little Blue was the most spirited of the three. She matched her brothers stride for stride as they romped around us. If Sam wasn't careful, he might find her coming home with me.

I realized I'd been daydreaming when Aunt Peg abruptly stopped speaking. I also realized that I'd missed something important. "I'm sorry. What did you say?"

"We were talking about Josie Mannerly," she informed me.

*We were?*

"You wondered if Lila's mystery caller might have been her landlady. Later, that got me to thinking about whether it might be possible to talk to Josie again after all these years. It occurred to me that perhaps I should try giving her a call."

I was torn between horror and delight. "Aunt Peg, you didn't!"

She smiled. Like the cat who'd had the canary and swallowed it whole. "First I waffled about it a bit—because who would be so rude as to invade the privacy of a famous recluse? But then I decided to do some nosing around, just to see how easy it would be to find a phone number."

"And?"

"It turned out that Josephine Mannerly has a listing in the New Canaan phone book. When I saw that, there was nothing left for me to do but dial it."

*"And?"* I demanded, when she paused again to rachet up the suspense.

"Josie didn't answer the phone, but I left a message. And she returned my call."

"She didn't!" I shrieked.

Aunt Peg chuckled at my response. "I was every bit as surprised as you are. I'd imagine she doesn't get too many phone calls. The people she knew in her heyday would have moved on with their lives after Josie left the social scene and went into seclusion."

"Did she remember you?" I asked breathlessly.

"Quite possibly not. After all, I was only one of many young debs who admired her in those days—but she was polite enough not to say so. Instead, she laughed and said, 'Nobody has called me Josie for years. Decades. Oh, that brings back such memories!'" Aunt Peg grinned. "After that, she and I got along splendidly."

The two black puppies went racing by. They'd found a small stick, and each was holding one end. Blue had her eye on her two brothers. I suspected she'd be stealing their prize from them shortly.

"Did you ask Josie what she knew about Lila Moran? And why the woman was living in her gatehouse?"

"I did not," Aunt Peg replied.

I stared at her in disbelief.

"Even better. I wangled an invitation for the two of us to visit her. At Josie's convenience, of course. Once we're there, I suspect we'll be able to ferret out all sorts of information."

I sighed happily. "Aunt Peg, you're a marvel."

"Yes, I know."

"Did she mention when a visit might be convenient?"

"Didn't I tell you that part?" Aunt Peg's eyes were twinkling. She knew perfectly well she hadn't. "We're expected this afternoon at four, for tea."

I spent the next several hours debating what one should wear to drink tea with a former Debutante of the Decade in the manor house of her posh estate. Nothing in my previous experience had prepared me to be able to answer that question. Google was no help either.

In the end, I put on a navy blue wool dress and knee-high leather boots. The outfit made me look reasonably presentable. Plus, in the event that the furnace in the main house worked as poorly as the one in the cottage, at least I would be warm. Faith, who'd observed my several changes of attire, seemed to approve. That was good enough for me.

Sam and the boys were out Christmas shop[
Aunt Peg came by to pick me up. I handed ou
butter biscuits to the Poodles and Bud, then advi
wily little mutt to behave himself while I was gon
previous year he'd waited until our Christmas tree
fully decorated, then scaled its branches like a cat.

Aunt Peg liked to drive fast and she made quick wo
of the trip to New Canaan. I directed her up Forest Glen
Lane and saw her eyes widen as we continued along the
tall wall that bordered the estate for a quarter mile before
we arrived at the gate. Aunt Peg had the code—why was
I not surprised?—and the majestic, iron-spiked, barrier
drew open before us.

When we came to the gatehouse, she braked the minivan and had a look. "That looks like the kind of place
where something dire should have happened," she decided. "I don't think I've ever seen a gloomier home. It's
a wonder anyone wanted to live in it at all."

"I'll be interested to hear how that came about," I
agreed. "Let's hope Josephine Mannerly is in a chatty
mood."

The driveway continued to wind its way through the
dense forest. We'd driven for several more minutes before we suddenly emerged from the trees and a sweeping
vista opened up before us.

A vast gently rolling lawn led to an enormous white
stone mansion. Gleaming softly in the winter sunlight,
the house was three stories tall. It had a mansard roof and
an elegant double staircase that led to a wide front por-
tico. There were more windows than I could count in the
time it took us to approach.

"Wow," I said. "That's impressive. If I lived here,
maybe I wouldn't want to leave either."

"I would," Aunt Peg retorted. "If only because leaving would offer me the pleasure of being able to return."

We climbed the steps to the front door and rang the doorbell. Moments later, the heavy door was opened by a maid in a severe black dress. She glanced at both of us briefly before her gaze settled on Aunt Peg.

"You must be Margaret Turnbull," she said. "Ms. Mannerly is expecting you. Please come inside."

"Margaret?" I said under my breath as we shed our coats. Nobody ever called Aunt Peg *Margaret*.

"A little formality seemed appropriate under the circumstances. Now mind your manners, or you'll make me wish I'd left you home."

That was enough to shut me up. We followed the maid down a spacious center hallway. When we reached the second set of double doors, the woman paused, her hands on the doorknobs.

"Ms. Mannerly has a degenerative condition. She will not stand to greet you. Instead she will expect you to cross the room and approach her. There are two chairs opposite her in front of the fireplace. Please make yourselves comfortable there."

The room Aunt Peg and I entered was a high-ceilinged library. Two of the walls were lined with bookshelves, and the floor was covered by a Savonnerie rug woven in vibrant jewel tones. Tall windows in the far wall provided a spectacular view of the panoramic park outside.

Josephine Mannerly was seated in an upholstered chair that faced the door. She had a book in her lap, but she carefully removed her reading glasses, then looked up and smiled as we approached. I knew she was just a few years older than Aunt Peg, but she appeared to be a much older woman.

Her white hair was gathered back off her face behind a wide headband, and her vividly colored Pucci dress would have been considered fashionable in the 1960s. Her legs, clad in support hose, were neatly crossed at the ankle. Josephine had a pale, heavily lined, face and clear blue eyes. Her hand trembled slightly as she extended it to Aunt Peg.

"You'll pardon me if I don't get up," she said. "Mildred will have explained why. You must be Margaret. Despite our snippet of shared history, you don't look familiar. After all these years, I dare say you probably wouldn't have recognized me either."

"Your eyes are exactly the same as I remember them," Aunt Peg replied diplomatically. "Didn't a society columnist once say they were the shade of a summer bluebird on the wing?"

"Oh my." Josephine laughed. "Your memory exceeds mine. Although if someone actually did say that, perhaps it's better off forgotten. Who is this young woman?"

"I'd like to introduce you to my niece, Melanie."

I stepped forward and shook her hand. It felt dry and weightless in mine. "I'm very pleased to meet you," I said.

"Yes, well, we'll see about that, won't we? Have a seat, both of you. Mildred will be in shortly with refreshments."

Josephine set her book and glasses down on a nearby table. She waited until we were seated before her gaze settled on Aunt Peg. "I agreed to see you because I was curious. And because for the first time in my very long life, I now find my name attached to a source of scandal. You were maddeningly indirect about your intentions on the phone. I suppose that was intentional—and it obviously worked, because here you are."

Aunt Peg nodded. She could probably be forgiven for looking rather pleased with herself.

"I don't see many people, and I don't suffer fools lightly," Josephine continued. "So let's get down to brass tacks. I'd like to hear what sort of information you think I might possess. And perhaps more importantly—should I choose to share what I know—what you intend to do with what I tell you."

# Chapter
# Twelve

There was a discreet knock on the door. Mildred entered the room, pushing a wooden trolley cart holding our tea. She set out delicate china cups and saucers on a low table between our chairs. A plate of wafer-thin vanilla cookies followed. The tea pot was large and looked heavy. It was made of Edwardian silver and there were teaspoons to match.

"I'll pour," Aunt Peg offered as Josephine dismissed the maid.

Mildred withdrew and we addressed ourselves to the food. The tea was Earl Grey, Aunt Peg's favorite. I preferred coffee, but I was willing to make do, especially since the vanilla cookies were divine.

After a minute had passed, Josephine looked up from her tea. "I'm waiting," she said pointedly.

"I was just gathering my thoughts," Aunt Peg said. She set down her teacup. "We've come today because a member of my extended family was acquainted with your tenant, Lila Moran. Claire had the misfortune to be the one who discovered her body and called the police. That chain of events led to Melanie's subsequent involvement in the investigation."

"Oh?" Josephine lifted a brow delicately. She turned in my direction. "I wasn't aware that you were a policewoman."

I swallowed a gulp of very hot tea. "I'm not. But Claire called me that morning. She asked me to come to your gatehouse for moral support."

"And yet your involvement lingers?"

"Melanie has a talent for solving mysteries," Aunt Peg told her.

Josephine's lips pursed. She did not look impressed. "What an unusual gift."

"I like asking questions," I said. "And taking bits of information—clues, you might call them—and weaving them together to form a pattern that tells a story."

"Whether or not you are talented at what you do remains to be seen," Josephine replied. "Ask your questions, and we will see if I choose to answer them."

All righty then. She'd gotten straight to the point. I would do the same.

"The woman who was living in your gatehouse was not who she said she was. There is no information about Lila Moran's past life that goes back more than five years. Before that, she appeared not to exist."

I watched the older woman's face as I spoke. Her composure never wavered. I'd expected the news to surprise her. Instead, Josephine Mannerly surprised me.

"You already knew that," I said.

"Of course I did," she replied calmly. "I knew everything about Lila. Otherwise she never would have been allowed on my property."

Aunt Peg and I shared a startled look.

"How did Lila come to be living in your gatehouse?" she asked.

"That's a long story. Much of it is old history now."

"I like old history," I said.

"I *lived* old history," Aunt Peg added drily.

"So you wish me to continue?"

Aunt Peg and I both nodded.

"Many years ago, when I was young, I had a suitor. This was before your time, Melanie, but Margaret will understand what I'm saying. In those days, very few women thought about having a career. We were expected to find a husband and start a family. That was what my parents wanted for me. It was what girls of my set aspired to."

Thank goodness times had changed, I thought.

"I met a man named William Schiff. He was five years older than me, very handsome, and terribly sophisticated." Josephine paused for a private smile. "Those things mattered to me. What mattered to my mother was that he came from a good family, had an Ivy League education, and was well employed in his father's business. All the pieces seemed to fit together perfectly. I thought we were a match made in heaven."

"It sounds as though things didn't turn out that way," I said.

"No, they did not. What I didn't know was that Billy was being pressured by his parents to court me. They wanted the prestige—and, of course, the money—that would come from having their son marry Joshua Mannerly's daughter."

"That could have been a problem with many of your suitors," Aunt Peg mentioned.

"Yes, although usually I was able to ferret out such ulterior motives. But with Billy, it was different. I fell head over heels in love."

"What happened?" I asked.

"Once we were engaged, Billy became moody and distant. I still had stars in my eyes, however. I thought everything would be fine once we were married. That was what I'd been brought up to believe."

"But you didn't get married, did you?" said Aunt Peg.

"No. A week before the wedding, Billy broke off our engagement. One day I thought we were blissfully happy. The next, everything I'd imagined we had together was gone. Billy asked for the ring back. It had been in his family for generations. For some reason, at the time that seemed like the worst blow of all."

"I remember there was a broken engagement." Aunt Peg thought back. "But I thought you were the one who ended it?"

"That was the story we told everyone. My mother insisted upon it. She sat Billy's father down and told him how things were going to be, and Mr. Schiff didn't dare say no."

Josephine hadn't been kidding when she said it was a long story. It seemed to me that we were still several decades away from Lila Moran and the mysterious gaps in her life. On the other hand, the vanilla wafers were superb. I helped myself to another and settled back in my chair.

"I was very young, and very naive, in those days," Josephine said.

"We all were," Aunt Peg agreed.

"I pictured myself as the spurned heroine in one of the romance novels I loved to read. Billy had been my knight in shining armor—or so I thought. I waited for him to come riding back to me on a white horse."

Good luck with that, I thought.

"A year later, Billy married someone else. A girl who had neither the class nor the connections that I possessed. By that time, my mother had died and I was on my own. I had come into my inheritance, but my family was gone. I was all alone. Up until that point, I had led rather a sheltered life. I wasn't accustomed to making my own decisions. And there was no one left who might have provided me with proper guidance."

"There hadn't been any other suitors?" Aunt Peg asked.

"Of course there were." The older woman waved a hand dismissively. "There were plenty of men who professed to be interested in me. But I'd grown cynical, and I never gave them a chance. I didn't have to, you see. By then I'd realized that I didn't need a man to take care of me."

"What does this have to do with Lila Moran?" I asked.

Aunt Peg shot me an annoyed look as Josephine frowned.

"I told you this was going to be a long story," she said. "You must let me tell it my way. Either that or you can finish your tea and go home."

"Yes, ma'am," I replied meekly. It looked as though we were going to be here awhile.

"Looking back now it seems foolish, but even after Billy married I kept tabs on what he was doing. I knew about his life with his new wife and their young daughter. I knew when his father died, and how Billy stepped up to take over the family business in his stead."

Josephine abruptly stopped speaking. She sipped her tea, then picked up a cookie and absently broke it into small pieces before setting it aside. This time I knew better than to try to hurry her along.

"Mind you, I'm not proud of what happened next," she said when she finally spoke. "In my own defense, I can only plead the arrogance of youth. Just when Billy thought he had everything—a successful career, a lovely child, and a wife who was wearing a ring that I thought belonged on *my* finger—I set about quite methodically to ruin him."

I sucked in a breath and slowly let it out. For a moment, the silence in the room was so complete that I could hear the ticking of a grandfather clock by the window.

"I assume you mean financially," Aunt Peg said.

"Of course that's what I mean," Josephine snapped. In her case, confession didn't appear to be good for the soul. "That was the instrument I had at my disposal. I put my father's money to use in aid of my own selfish cause. What I did was wrong, but I'm not going to apologize for it. I was headstrong and foolish, and I lashed out. It was a poor decision, but it was one I made years ago."

"Let me guess," Aunt Peg ventured. "Was Lila Moran Billy Schiff's daughter?"

"You're quite smart, aren't you?" Josephine regarded her with admiration. "Yes, that's exactly it."

"I still don't get it," I said. "How did Lila end up here?"

"I suspect that all these years later, Josephine set out to make amends," Aunt Peg told me.

The older woman nodded, then continued her story. "After Billy lost his company, he began to drink. After alcohol, he turned to drugs. Things spiraled downward from there. Billy and his wife were divorced, so he lost his family too. My revenge was complete and I expected to feel satisfaction—but instead my intemperate actions led only to a crushing sense of remorse."

"I should hope so," I muttered. Aunt Peg kicked me under the table.

I jumped slightly in my seat as Josephine trained a beady gaze on me. "Have you never made a mistake?" she demanded.

"I've made many," I admitted. "Although not one of that magnitude."

"Then you're lucky," she shot back. "But you're still young. It may yet happen."

I hoped not. I couldn't imagine wanting to manipulate someone else's life like that.

"Billy's wife married two more times," Josephine said. "Lila had a difficult upbringing. She was arrested for the first time when she was still in high school. Shoplifting became petty theft, then grand theft. She seemed to have a hard time keeping her hands off of other people's possessions. Eventually she served a year in jail. When she got out, her past missteps had made her virtually unemployable."

"That would have been five years ago," I guessed.

"Precisely. At that point I decided to step in and see if I could use my considerable resources to turn things around for her. Lila had already built herself a new identity by the time I contacted her. That sort of subterfuge certainly wouldn't have been *my* idea, though it did smooth things along. After that, I made sure that Lila always had a decent job and a place to live. It hasn't been easy. There have been several setbacks along the way, but I've done my best to keep nudging her in the right direction."

"So eventually you found her a job nearby and moved her into your gatehouse."

"I'm not as young as I used to be," Josephine pointed out unnecessarily. "Nor as healthy. After Lila had been let go from her previous place of employment, I decided it made sense to put her somewhere close, where I could keep an eye on her. I thought it would be easier to keep her out of trouble that way."

"And yet this is where she ended up dead," Aunt Peg pointed out.

Josephine nodded but didn't reply.

"Do you have any thoughts about that?" I prompted.

"I most certainly do not," she said sharply. "Peebles, the man who looks after the estate, has been in contact with the local police. He assures me they are doing everything they can to solve this horrible crime."

"But you haven't spoken to them?"

"No, of course not. Why would I do that? Peebles is handling everything. That's his job."

"Mr. Peebles was also supposed to be taking care of Lila's cottage," I mentioned.

"Yes. What of it?"

"When was the last time you saw the place?" Aunt Peg asked. "It looks as though it was falling down around her ears."

"That can't be right." Josephine stared at the two of us.

"I'm afraid it is," I told her. "A friend of Lila's told me she was afraid of your caretaker."

"Afraid? That's preposterous. Peebles wouldn't hurt a fly."

"I also heard that he wanted something from Lila," I said. "Do you have any idea what that might have been?"

"None whatsoever," Josephine stated firmly. "Peebles has been with me a long time. He thinks he knows what's best for me. Perhaps that leads him to be a bit overprotective when it comes to looking out for my interests."

"Territorial sounds more like it," Aunt Peg muttered.

"The gatehouse had been empty for years. After all, it's not as though I have many visitors. But Peebles assured me that he'd fixed the place up properly before Lila moved in. I don't know how it could be in such a state of disrepair."

It sounded as though Peebles was often quick to assure the older woman that all was well. I wondered how often Josephine had checked to see whether or not he was telling her the truth. When I asked her that, she stiffened in her seat. Intrusive as our earlier questions had been, this time I'd gone too far.

"Peebles isn't just an employee. He's also a relative. Distant, to be sure, but one of the very few that I have left," she said in a tight voice. "I am quite certain he wouldn't do anything to undermine my wishes."

Even with the fire blazing beside us, the atmosphere in the room had suddenly cooled. Aunt Peg took that as her cue. She rose to her feet.

"Thank you for allowing us to visit this afternoon. We've taken up enough of your time," she said, taking the woman's hand in both of hers. "It's been lovely to see you. I hope we'll have another opportunity to get together soon."

"I'd like that," Josephine replied, her good manners as ingrained as Aunt Peg's.

"If there's ever anything you need . . . ," Aunt Peg offered.

Josephine shook her head. "No, there wouldn't be. I'm aware that those in the outside world who remember me are puzzled by my lifestyle. But I'm not a prisoner in this house. I live this way by choice. Why would I ever need to leave when everything I want is right here?"

Mildred showed us out. Aunt Peg and I waited until we were back in her minivan before speaking again.

"Imagine ruining someone's life out of spite," I said.

"To have that much money and choose to use it in such a destructive way." Aunt Peg sounded shaken as she turned the key and put the van into gear. "I don't suppose I'll ever understand *that*. But at least we solved the mystery of Lila's past."

"But unfortunately that doesn't lead us any closer to knowing who killed her," I said. "Or why."

# Chapter
# Thirteen

On Monday Sam had meetings in the city all day. That made it my turn to get everybody up and fed, and to make sure that both Davey and his homework got on the school bus. Then I dropped Kevin off at preschool.

After that, all I had to do was wait an hour for the stores to open. Then it was time for some serious Christmas shopping. Due to extenuating circumstances, I was way behind on my gift buying. Today was my day to remedy that deficit. Since I had time to kill before I could go wear out my credit cards, I decided to take the dogs for a run.

That idea went out the window when the doorbell rang. I wasn't expecting anybody. I'm almost never expecting anyone. But that never seems to stop random people from showing up at my door at all hours.

This visitor was a real surprise. And not necessarily a good one. I opened the door anyway.

"Mr. Peebles," I said. "What are you doing here?"

Before he could answer, all five Standard Poodles came swarming out the open doorway. Only Bud was missing. He doesn't usually pass up anything of interest, so I wondered what kind of trouble the little miscreant was getting into elsewhere.

There was no opportunity to look for him now, however, because Hank Peebles had thrown up his hands and gone stumbling backward off my front step. A strangled sound came out of his mouth. Judging by the expression on his face, he thought death was possibly imminent.

Karma's a bitch, isn't it?

"Don't like dogs?" I inquired pleasantly.

"Those aren't dogs," he growled. "They look like bears."

Maybe the Poodles' freshly blown-out coats did make them look bigger than they actually were. But not *that* big. Definitely not bears.

"Nope," I told him. "They're Poodles. And this is their house."

I added that last part in case it might discourage him from prolonging this encounter. And also because I didn't exactly trust him. If Peebles had stopped by with something stupid in mind, I wanted him to be clear about the fact that my peeps and I had him outnumbered.

"We need to talk," he said. "Can I come in?" He gazed around at the Poodles, as though he wasn't entirely sure that was a wise idea.

Good, I thought. That made two of us.

"I guess so." It wasn't an invitation.

Peebles stepped past me through the doorway. The

Standard Poodles followed him inside. As he stood in the hallway, the dogs continued to crowd around his legs. I continued not to discourage them from doing so. The dogs were only being friendly, but apparently Peebles didn't know that. And I had no desire to enlighten him.

I closed the door behind us and asked, "What do you want?"

Peebles was wearing the same tweed cap he'd had on the last time I saw him. Once inside the house, he reached up and swept it off his head. When his hand returned to his side, Augie stepped in close to sniff the cloth cap. Peebles cringed away from the big black dog.

Darn it. I wanted him to be intimidated. But the guy actually looked afraid.

"They won't hurt you," I said reluctantly.

"How do you know that?"

"Because they're my dogs and I trained them. They only attack on command."

*Just kidding.* But Peebles paled slightly. The cap twisted in his hands. Clearly the man had never met a Standard Poodle before.

"Look Ms. Travis," he said. "I'm not your enemy."

"Are you sure?" My brow lifted. "Because that's not what it seemed like the last time we met."

"Yeah, well, that wasn't the best of circumstances, considering that you and your friend had just broken into a house that's in my care."

"I wouldn't admit that so freely if I were you. That gatehouse doesn't look like it's been in anybody's care for years. Lila said she could never get you to come and fix things."

"Lila said a lot of things." Peebles smirked. "I wouldn't take her word as gospel on any of them."

"The police must have questioned you about her murder," I said.

"They did," he grumbled. "Not that there was a need. It's not like I knew anything about it."

"I knew something." I stared at him across the small space. "I told the police that Lila was afraid of you. That she had something you wanted."

"What?" I'd expected Peebles to react angrily. Instead he looked perplexed. "I don't know what you're talking about. Who told you that?"

"A woman named Karen Clauson. Her husband worked with Lila."

He shook his head. "I never met that woman. I have no idea where she'd come up with an idea like that. The only thing I wanted from Lila Moran was for her to go away and leave Ms. Mannerly in peace."

"And now she has," I pointed out.

"I had nothing to do with Lila's death," Peebles snarled. "Don't go trying to pin that on me. I didn't do anything to her."

The Poodles had grown bored listening to us talk. They'd laid down on the wooden floor around us. But now, hearing the menace in Peebles' tone, Tar and Faith jumped to their feet. The two Poodles looked at me questioningly. I patted my thigh, and both big dogs moved to stand between me and the caretaker.

*Good dogs.*

Peebles' eyes tracked the Poodles' movements. When they took up their new positions, he backed as far away from me as he could. The length of his body pressed against the wall behind him.

"It doesn't sound as though you did anything to help Lila either," I said.

"That woman didn't need my help." Peebles was still angry. But when Tar shifted his stance, the man glanced down at the male dog and moderated his tone. "Lila knew all about how to look out for herself. Which is more than you can say for Ms. M. The boss is a great lady, but she's led a secluded life. She doesn't always understand how the real world works. All I was trying to do was protect her."

*Right.* I crossed my arms over my chest and waited for further explanation.

"Okay, maybe I didn't always get around to making repairs," he admitted. "Maybe it occurred to me that if the furnace was smoking and the roof leaked, Lila might decide to pick up and move on to someone else's cushier digs. That's what her kind does. They're users, always on the lookout for someone to take care of them."

"How would you know that?"

"I've got eyes and ears, don't I? I pay attention to what goes on around me, especially when it concerns Ms. M or the estate. So I've seen the kind of people who come and go at that gatehouse since Lila moved in and made herself at home. Bunch of lowlifes, if you ask me."

*Pot meet kettle*, I thought.

Peebles frowned. "Except the one guy. Drove a red Ferrari, for Pete's sake. Classic midlife crisis car. I had to admire his taste in wheels, even if he was stooping to boink the help."

"The help?" I was confused. "What help?"

"It's my job to know what's happening on the estate so I looked up his license plate. The guy was Lila's boss. He's been showing up at the gatehouse once or twice a week for the past six months. The guys she hung out with before him didn't have much staying power, but this one sure did."

"Who are you talking about?" I asked. "What boss?"

"You know him," Peebles told me. "You were talking about his wife earlier. Guy named Clauson, George Clauson."

My stomach dropped. "He was having an affair with Lila?"

"I just said that, didn't I? That woman, she had him wrapped around her little finger. Probably thought he was going to be her ticket to a better life. And who knows? Maybe he would have been. Guy must have really been into her."

*Damn*, I thought. How had I missed that?

"Did you tell Detective Hronis about that?" I asked.

"Sure." Peebles shrugged. "Last week. I answered every question he had. He said he'd look into what I'd told him, along with everything else."

"Someone needs to tell him again," I said.

"Not me." With an eye on the Poodles, Peebles stepped away from the wall. In two steps he was back at the door. He reached for the knob and turned it. "But if you think it matters, go ahead."

"I will."

I'd call the detective just as soon as Peebles left. But meanwhile, I still had no idea what he was doing at my house. And now he was about to go. He'd drawn the door open and was ready to walk out.

"Wait," I said. "Why did you come?"

Peebles stopped and turned back. "Oh yeah. With your dogs attacking me like that, I almost forgot."

He reached a hand inside his jacket and my breath caught. I hoped he didn't have a weapon in there. Then he withdrew his hand and held it out to me. I couldn't see what he was holding, but I found myself reaching for it anyway.

Something cool and lightweight dropped into my palm. I looked down at it and blinked in surprise. Claire's gold bangle.

"I found it on the ground near where your friend parked her car," Peebles told me. "I know she wanted it back. I figured you could give it to her."

I looked up at him and swallowed. Maybe I needed to reassess a few things. "Thank you for returning the bracelet. Claire will be thrilled to have it back."

"It's nothing. Like I said, Ms. Travis, I'm not your enemy."

No, I supposed not.

I waited until Peebles had driven away before I grabbed my phone and called Detective Hronis. I had to wait two minutes for someone to find him. Or for him to decide whether or not he wanted to speak to me. Either one was possible. By the time the detective picked up, I was drumming my fingers on the bannister impatiently.

"Detective Hronis," he barked. "Ms. Travis?"

"Yes, I'm here," I said. "I was just talking to Hank Peebles. You know, the caretaker at the Mannerly estate?"

"Yes, I'm familiar with Mr. Peebles." He waited for me to continue.

"He told me that Lila Moran was having an affair with George Clauson."

"We're aware of that."

"Did you ask him about it?"

"Ms. Travis, I'm not required to keep you informed of police activity."

"No, of course not." I walked around the newel post and sat down on a step. The Poodles were spread out on the floor, listening as I talked. They probably understood me better than Detective Hronis did. "But George Clauson's wife, Karen—"

"We talked to her too, Ms. Travis." He was beginning to sound bored.

"Karen's position as George's wife and her standing in the community mean everything to her. If his relationship with Lila put those things at risk, or if she was afraid that George might leave her . . ."

My voice trailed away. I was waiting for Detective Hronis to connect the dots, just as I had. Several long seconds ticked by in silence.

"We've considered that, Ms. Travis, and we're looking into it," Hronis replied finally. "But right now, all we have is speculation. Mrs. Clauson told us she was aware of her husband's extramarital activities. And both of them told us that he had already ended the affair before Lila Moran was killed."

"And you believed them?" I asked skeptically.

"Let's just say I'm keeping an open mind. But as I said, this is all just conjecture. We would need some kind of proof before pursuing this line of inquiry further."

"I could talk to Chris Sanchez again," I said. "Maybe she knows something."

There was another pause before the detective spoke. "I'll repeat what I told you before, Ms. Travis. This is police business. The best thing would be for you to put it out of your mind. I wouldn't want you to do anything stupid."

"Nor would I," I replied. But that didn't mean I wasn't going to talk to Chris again.

"He didn't care about what I had to say," I told the dogs glumly when we'd severed the connection. "Thank goodness for you guys. You always pay attention to me."

Faith and Eve hopped up. Augie was already on his feet. The Poodle group was ready to play. I still had time to get in a run before heading out to shop. But first I needed to find Bud. What the heck could he be up to that was more interesting than a visitor in the front hall? No doubt it was something nefarious.

Since it was Bud we were talking about, it probably involved food. So I headed to the kitchen first. The pantry door was standing open. Suspicious noises were coming from within. I walked around and had a look.

Bud was lying on the floor next to a forty pound bag of kibble. He'd managed to chew a small hole in the bottom of the bag. Now he was using his tongue to pull out the kibble piece by piece. You know, because we never fed him, poor thing.

"Bud, cut that out!" I said.

He looked up at me and wagged his tail. *Happy! Happy!*

"You are not happy," I said firmly. "You're in trouble."

*Happy! Happy!*

Dammit, it was a good thing he was so cute.

I dragged him out of the pantry. Then I went back and taped up the bottom of the bag. It wasn't a perfect patch, but it would do.

Five minutes later I was finally getting ready to go for that run when my phone rang. I snatched it up. Maybe it was Detective Hronis calling back to tell me I was brilliant.

No such luck. It was Claire.

"Hey," I said. "Good news! I've got your missing bracelet."

"That's nice," she replied. *Nice?* "But I don't care about that right now. Can we talk?"

"Sure. What's up?"

"Not on the phone." Her voice sounded shaky. "In person."

"I guess so," I said slowly. There went my run. And my Christmas shopping. But something didn't feel right. "Claire, are you okay?"

"Yes," she replied. I wasn't reassured. "But I need to see you. Now."

"I can do that. Where are you?"

"I'm at the gatehouse."

"What?" Thoughts whirling, I nearly tripped over Bud. "What are you doing there?"

"I can't explain. I just need you to come."

I was already dodging around Poodles as I hurried from the kitchen. "Claire, what's going on?"

"Just come."

Luckily I had the phone pressed tight against my ear. Because that meant I heard her slip out the word "not" in a breathy whisper before saying out loud, "Alone."

*Oh crap*, I thought.

"Claire, talk to me!" I cried.

She didn't reply. The connection had already ended.

# Chapter
# Fourteen

If I took the back roads between North Stamford and New Canaan, I could be at the Mannerly estate in ten minutes. I called Detective Hronis on the way. This time, it took even longer for him to come on the line.

"Pick up, pick up, pick up!" I muttered, my fingers tapping on the steering wheel.

By the time he finally did, I was so stressed that I wasted another couple of minutes trying to make him understand the urgency of the matter.

"I thought I told you the gatehouse was off-limits," he said.

"That's not the point," I almost yelled. "Claire isn't there by choice. I know something's wrong. I'm on my way there right now to find out what."

"If you think there's trouble, the last thing you should do is go running toward it," the detective told me.

How could he remain so calm when what I wanted to do was scream in frustration?

"Somebody has to!" I snapped.

I tossed the phone on the other seat and drove. The Volvo's tires squealed as I made the turn onto Forest Glen. Not much farther now.

As I flew along beside the Mannerly estate's high wall, a car came up behind me. A plain sedan with an angry detective at the wheel. Beggars couldn't be choosers. I'd have preferred a happy detective, but at least he'd come.

I skidded to a stop in front of the iron gate. It was closed.

Detective Hronis pulled up behind me. He rolled down his window. "You drive like a maniac," he said. "Move your car out of the way and get in. I have the gate code."

I hurried to obey and was already seated beside him before the gate began to swing open.

"If this is a false alarm, I'm going to give you a speeding ticket," Hronis informed me.

"It isn't."

He glanced at me across the seat as we rolled up beside the gatehouse. "How can you be so sure?"

I pointed to a black Mercedes coupe parked behind the cottage. "Because that isn't Claire's car. Whatever she's doing here, she didn't come because she wanted to."

"Wait in the car," said Hronis.

Fat chance of that. I had jumped out and was heading toward the gatehouse before he had his seat belt unfastened. Apparently, once motivated, the detective could move quickly. When I reached the door, he was right beside me. Hronis held out an arm to bar my way.

"I'll go in first." He slanted a glare my way. "Or are you going to argue with that too?"

I stepped to one side. The detective lifted a hand and knocked on the wooden door. "Ms. Travis, it's Detective Hronis. Are you in there?"

For a moment, there was no response. The detective and I shared an uneasy look. He raised his hand to knock again.

Abruptly a shriek rent the air. The hair on the back of my neck lifted. A chill slipped down my spine. I froze in place but the detective's reflexes were quicker. He shoved me away, then leapt sideways himself.

We landed on the hard ground together just as I heard a loud roar. The sound was so unexpected that it took me a moment to realize what it was. A gunshot. A hole blasted through the wooden door above us. Shards of splintered wood came raining down.

"Claire!" I screamed. I started to scramble up. All I knew was that I had to get inside the cottage.

Detective Hronis had a different idea. He grabbed my arm in a viselike grip, dragged me back to the car, and shoved me down behind it. "Don't move," he said. When I nodded, he crawled inside the sedan and called for backup.

"Claire's in there," I said when he was finished.

"Who's she with?" he demanded.

"I don't know. She didn't say." My voice wobbled. "She probably couldn't say."

The detective's radio came on. He talked some more. I could already hear the sound of sirens in the distance. He turned back to me and said, "They ran the plate. It's Karen Clauson."

"She has Claire," I said. "And a gun. We have to do something."

"We are doing something, Ms. Travis. We're doing everything we can, as quickly as we can. In just a few minutes, we'll have the gatehouse surrounded. A hostage negotiator is on the way."

A phalanx of cars came flying up the driveway toward us. They stopped a short distance away. Doors slammed. Officers got out. They were wearing body armor and they were armed.

My body shook uncontrollably as I sat on the ground behind the detective's sedan. I wasn't just cold; I was in shock. Things like this didn't happen in suburban Connecticut. It was like watching a scene from a movie. How had things escalated so quickly?

Detective Hronis rose to his knees and gazed at the gatehouse through the windows of the car. All was quiet. Nothing moved. "Stay here," he said.

He went to confer with the other police, who'd assembled behind us. I received a few curious glances. Other than that, they all ignored me. I supposed that was fair. I was the one who'd gotten them into this mess.

Several of the officers left the group. I watched as they fanned out around the gatehouse. While they were doing that, Detective Hronis donned protective body armor. Someone handed him a bullhorn. He lifted it to his lips.

"Karen Clauson," he said. "We know you're in there. We need you to open the door and come out now with your hands up."

There was no response. Detective Hronis didn't look perturbed. He calmly repeated his message. I chewed on my lip, waiting with the others.

A minute later, Hronis tried again. "We have the gatehouse surrounded," he announced. "The only way out is through that door, with your hands up. You're only making things worse for yourself, Karen. Let's end this peacefully before something happens that we all regret."

Several regrettable things had already happened, I thought. Of course, it wouldn't help to remind anyone of that. All I could do was keep my head down, stay out of the way, and pray for Claire's safety.

I was still sitting with my back against the sedan, so when I heard the sound of a door scraping open, it came from behind me. What *was* in my line of vision were half a dozen police officers who immediately snapped to attention. I spun around, got up on my knees, and peered through the car window.

Karen Clauson was standing silhouetted in the doorway. "I'm coming out," she said.

Detective Hronis nodded. He still looked remarkably calm. As if he'd never expected any other outcome.

"Put down your weapon," he said. "And raise your hands in the air."

Karen complied.

"Now slowly walk toward us."

After that, everything that happened felt like one long blur of frantic activity. Karen was quickly taken into custody. As several officers moved to surround her, I was already up and running. When Detective Hronis entered the gatehouse, I was right behind him.

Claire was in the kitchen, lying slumped on the floor. Her eyes were closed; her face was pale as milk. My stomach plummeted—and then I realized that I didn't see any blood. She hadn't been shot.

Instead, there was a purpling bruise on Claire's forehead. A knot the size of a golf ball was already forming.

Hronis knelt down beside her and felt for a pulse. "Strong and steady," he said, looking up at me. "Although I'm sure she'll have a nasty headache when she wakes up."

The ambulance was at the end of the driveway. By the time the paramedics reached the cottage, Claire was starting to regain consciousness. Against the detective's wishes, she wanted to sit up. As I held her steady, she looked around in confusion.

Her hand lifted to touch the bump on her head. "Where's Karen? What did she do to me?"

"It looks like she knocked you out," I said.

Claire blinked slowly. "She must have hit me when I tried to warn you not to come inside. Karen made me call you. She had a gun."

"We know all about that," Detective Hronis told her. "You can relax now, Ms. Travis. She doesn't have the gun anymore. My men have taken her into custody."

I took her cold hand in mine and squeezed hard. "Claire, tell us what happened."

She frowned, as though it hurt to think back. "Karen called me this morning. She said she'd made a mistake when she'd told me she didn't need my services anymore. She wanted to talk to me about an upcoming event. And dummy that I was, I fell for that."

"You couldn't have known," I told her.

"All Karen really wanted to do was pump me for information about how much you knew," Claire said. I was glad to see that her color was starting to return. "I told her you were good at solving mysteries. And that I was sure you'd get to the bottom of things, because you always do. That must have made her panic, because she took out a gun. She brought me here and made me call you."

There was a sudden commotion in the doorway. We all

looked up. Karen was standing there. Her hands were cuffed behind her back, and there was an officer on either side of her. She wasn't wearing a coat and she was shivering from the cold. Ask me if I cared. I curled an arm around Claire's shoulders protectively.

Hronis lifted a brow at the interruption.

"She said she had something to say," Office Jenkins told him.

"Go ahead," the detective told her.

Karen ignored him. Instead, she looked at me. "This is all your fault," she spat out.

"How do you figure that?"

"If you hadn't kept coming around, asking your stupid questions, and sticking your nose where it didn't belong, everything would have been fine."

I snuck a glance at Detective Hronis. He looked like a man who'd just swallowed something distasteful. But he had the sense to remain silent and let the conversation play out.

"Except that Lila Moran would have been dead," I said mildly.

"That bitch was sleeping with my husband. Always telling him how handsome he was, and how smart." Karen's face was mottled red with rage. "She wouldn't leave George alone. She told him that just like his car, he needed a newer model woman. She said I was *too old* for him, can you imagine?"

A gesture of solidarity seemed necessary, so I shook my head. "After all the work you'd done to keep yourself in shape for him too."

My sarcasm must have gone right over Karen's head, because she nodded in agreement.

"I guess Lila deserved what happened to her," I said.

"Damn right she did," Karen swore. Then she glared at me. "Except that you got in the way. When you wanted to meet with me for a *second* time, I realized I was in trouble. You pretended the conversation was about Claire, but I knew you knew."

She was giving me more credit than I deserved, I thought sadly. If only I'd been that quick on the uptake, this whole crazy episode could have been avoided.

"I haven't been able to sleep since," she snapped. "I knew I had to fix things *again*. I had to fix you."

"Why drag Claire into it?" I asked.

Karen's gaze dropped. She looked at Claire without remorse. "I knew you two were close," she said with a shrug. "I figured you'd do whatever she asked."

"You're right," I replied. "I would."

I heard Claire sigh. She reached out and wrapped an arm around my waist in a sideways hug. But I had one more question for Karen.

"Why here?"

She looked surprised. "Are you kidding me? Why *not* here? This cottage is a dump. It looks like the kind of place where people would die. Besides, I thought if two more women came to grief in the same place Lila did, the police would devote their resources to checking out this weird abandoned property."

Karen glanced at Detective Hronis dismissively. "And that would direct their attention away from me."

The property wasn't abandoned, but I didn't think Josephine Mannerly would appreciate my issuing a correction. Plus, only an idiot would be dumb enough to insult the police while she was standing there wearing their handcuffs. Detective Hronis obviously felt the same way.

"That's enough," he told the officers. "Get her out of here."

He and I helped Claire to her feet. She was examined by the paramedics and told she had a probable concussion. They recommended that she see her personal physician, and I assured them I would take her myself. I felt incredibly lucky that the injury wasn't worse.

# Epilogue

After all that excitement died down, I finally got a chance to finish my Christmas shopping. Claire bounced back quickly. Over her objections, I also helped her complete her remaining holiday shopping assignments. Under the circumstances, it seemed like the least I could do.

Aunt Peg invited our family to her house for Christmas dinner. I knew she didn't cook, so I wondered what kind of alternative plan she'd come up with. I hoped it didn't involve me and an apron. But when we arrived, the table in her dining room was set with polished silver and a linen tablecloth, and the heavenly smell of roasting turkey filled the air.

There were more presents under Aunt Peg's Christmas

tree for both Kevin and Davey. After they were opened and admired, the three Aussie puppies were brought into the living room to be played with. Meanwhile, we grown-ups relaxed in front of the fireplace with mugs of heavily spiked eggnog.

"I asked Josie Mannerly to join us for dinner," Aunt Peg mentioned.

Sam and I stared at each other in surprise.

"Is she coming?" I asked eagerly.

Aunt Peg laughed. "Gracious, no. The woman's a recluse. She never leaves her house. I just couldn't resist asking, to see what she'd say."

"After everything she went through with Lila Moran, she's probably relieved to be finished dealing with out-siders," Sam said.

"As it turns out, she's not entirely finished," Aunt Peg told us. "I happened to remember that Josie was a dog lover. Years ago she and her mother had a pair of Pek-ingese they took everywhere. The dogs became nearly as famous as their owners. Of course, on an estate that size, she might want a larger dog."

My head swiveled her way. "Aunt Peg, what did you do?"

"I merely made the obvious suggestion."

I glanced down at the puppies, who were rolling around the floor with Kevin. They'd grown again since the last time I saw them. An adult Australian Shepherd would be tall enough to rest its head comfortably in Josie's lap while she sat in her chair.

"Did she want a male or female?" Sam asked with a smile. "A black puppy or a blue?"

"Josie's always been a bit spoiled," Aunt Peg said. "She isn't used to having to make choices. So there was no need for her to start now. Once those puppies are old enough to be inoculated and have their training started, the two boys will be going to live in the former carriage house with Hank Peebles. Blue will reside in the mansion with Josie."

"That sounds like a wonderful solution all the way around," said Sam.

"I thought so," Aunt Peg agreed with satisfaction. "Now, who's ready to eat?"

Davey looked up from his seat on the floor. "Who cooked?"

"Shush," I told him. "That isn't polite."

"But a sensible inquiry nonetheless." Aunt Peg slipped him a wink. "Village Catering did the honors. Does that meet with your approval?"

Davey and Kevin both nodded. Even Sam looked relieved.

"Everything you do meets with our approval," he said.

"Don't tell her that." I laughed. "She'll get a big head."

"Bigger than I already have?" Aunt Peg was amused. "That hardly seems possible. Now hurry up, you lot. Last one to the table doesn't get a drumstick."

The boys each picked up a puppy. Aunt Peg nabbed the third. The three of them left the room together, moving like people on a mission.

Sam and I stood up to follow. Aunt Peg had lowered the lights and the decorations on her Christmas tree glistened in the firelight. Their soft glow was reflected in the windows. It all looked so beautiful that I just wanted to pause briefly to appreciate the moment.

Sam felt the same way. He stepped closer and slipped an arm around my shoulders.

"It's been a great year," I said.

"We've been very lucky." He leaned down and kissed the top of my head. "And next year will be even better."

# Author's Note

The background for this book was partially inspired by the story of Huguette Clark, a woman of immense wealth who shut herself away in her New York City apartment after the deaths of her sister and her parents. She spent the remainder of her life—nearly fifty years—speaking to very few people and seeing almost no one. Among the grand properties Huguette owned (and never visited again) were Bellosguardo, a twenty-three-acre beachfront estate in Santa Barbara, California, and Le Beau Chateau, a secluded mansion on fifty acres of wooded land in New Canaan, Connecticut.

*Standard Poodle owner Melanie Travis is an excellent judge of dogs—and people. But what happens when an unnamed killer emerges at one of the fiercest all-breed competitions ever?*

As Greenwich, Connecticut, slows down during a bitterly cold February, Melanie and her spunky Aunt Peg head to the city that never sleeps for the Westminster Kennel Club Dog Show at Madison Square Garden. Aunt Peg can't wait to demonstrate her judging chops on national TV, even after being hounded by frustrating mishaps—all seemingly orchestrated by Victor Durbin, an ousted Paugussett Poodle Club member with a bone to pick. But the bright lights of the show ring grow dim when Victor is found murdered, and she's the one topping the suspect list . . .

Driven to solve the crime on her aunt's behalf, Melanie fetches hair-raising clues about the victim. Victor didn't score many friends with his unethical breeding practices, sketchy puppy café, and penchant for mercilessly scamming others to get ahead. He burned so many bridges that his own business partner admits to being delighted by news of his death. It appears Victor finally toyed with the wrong person, and as Melanie digs up more chilling evidence, she realizes that exonerating Aunt Peg means confronting a murderer who's in it to win it . . .

**Please turn the page for an exciting sneak peek of
Laurien Berenson's next
Melanie Travis Canine Mystery
GAME OF DOG BONES
now on sale wherever print and e-books are sold!**

# Chapter
# One

Westminster Kennel Club Dog Show is the pinnacle. For two days in early February, New York City is the only place for the country's best show dogs to be. This event is the American dog world's biggest stage. The top handlers, owners, and exhibitors are all there, eager to test each other's mettle as their dogs compete for the ultimate prize: Westminster Best in Show.

Throughout the year, there are dog shows with larger entries. And ones held at easier venues. There are certainly shows with better weather. But none captivate the imagination the way Westminster does. None possess its enduring allure.

The Westminster Dog Show is the second oldest continuous sporting event in the country. First held in 1887, it began before the formation of the American Kennel

Club. The show has always made its home at Madison Square Garden, and over the years judging has had to persevere through such disruptions as blizzards and transit strikes.

Westminster isn't just the oldest dog show in the country, however; it's also the most prestigious. Dogs with connections to famous athletes, rock stars, and a British monarch have all competed there. This is the event that every dog lover wants to attend, and every exhibitor wants to win.

The individual breed competition now takes place on Monday and Tuesday at two West Side piers. But at night the show returns to the Garden for judging of the seven groups and Best in Show. Dogs and their handlers are all perfectly groomed, on their toes, and ready to perform.

There's a sudden hush, quickly followed by a burst of appreciative applause, when the day's winners gait into the big ring for the first time. The air in the arena feels electric. Clearly something special is happening.

Westminster has never forgotten its roots as a sporting event for serious dog fanciers. But it has also evolved into spectacular entertainment for a national audience. The result is pure magic for dog lovers.

"Magic," I murmured. I was staring out the car window at the passing scenery, which was currently the Bronx.

It was the Sunday before the start of the Westminster Dog Show and we were on our way to Manhattan. My husband, Sam, was driving. My Aunt Peg—also known as Margaret Turnbull, esteemed dog show judge and breeder of some of the best Standard Poodles the breed had ever known—was sitting beside him in the front of the SUV.

I'd been relegated to the rear seat, which was no surprise. Aunt Peg was clever and astute. She loved a good argument and preferred her own opinions to anyone else's. But mostly she liked to be in charge. That feat was more easily accomplished from the position with the best view.

Aunt Peg's gaze flitted to the window. We were driving past a factory that had seen better days. Probably during the previous century. "Magic?" She turned to look at me over her shoulder. "This?"

"No, I was thinking about Westminster."

"Of course you were thinking about Westminster." She settled back in her seat happily. "Who wouldn't be?"

Two years earlier, Aunt Peg had received the coveted letter inviting her to judge this year's Non-Sporting Group. She told us later that she'd shrieked out loud and danced around the room. Aunt Peg is seventy years old, nearly six feet tall, and not known for her agility. I wish I'd been there to see that.

"Your judging assignment is a huge honor," Sam said. He kept his blue eyes trained on the road but he was following the conversation. Sam and I have been married for six years and he's always been able to manage Aunt Peg better than I do.

"It is indeed," Aunt Peg agreed. "I only hope I prove worthy of the faith the Westminster board has placed in me."

"You will," I told her. "You're an excellent judge."

"I know that." Lack of confidence has never been a problem for Aunt Peg. "But Westminster is more than a dog show. It's a grand spectacle for the dog-owning masses.

Not to mention a wonderful opportunity for good canine public relations. The show's television audience numbers in the millions."

"Don't tell me you're nervous about being on TV," I said.

"No, that part of it is just a distraction. My job is about the dogs—not the lights and the cameras."

"Yes, but you'll still have to get your hair and make-up done beforehand," I teased. Over Aunt Peg's objections, both appointments had already been made.

"That's just a lot of pointless fuss and bother," she grumbled. "Everybody already knows what I look like."

"Not in TV land," Sam said with a grin. "You know, the dog-owning masses?"

"You're not helping." Aunt Peg reached over and smacked his arm. "I'm already well aware that this as- signment is a big deal. But what I'm feeling about it isn't nerves. It's anticipation. I can't wait to get my hands on all those wonderful dogs. But at the same time, I want to be sure that I rise to their level. My judging must be every bit as good as the champions in front of me."

Sam and I nodded. We could both understand that.

"Not only that, but when you look at the list of Poodle breeders who have judged this group before me, I am fol- lowing in some very distinguished footsteps," she contin- ued. "Heaven forbid I let the side down."

"That's not going to happen," Sam told her. "If you weren't every bit as good as those judges who've pre- ceded you, the Paugussett Poodle Club wouldn't have asked you to conduct today's seminar on evaluating Poo- dles."

"Yes, well, that's another thing," Aunt Peg said with a frown. "Before I can even get to tomorrow evening's show, first I have to make it through the rest of the week-end."

From my perch in the middle of the backseat I could see that her hands were fidgeting in her lap. Whatever she was doing, Aunt Peg almost always had one of her beloved Standard Poodles at her side. Today we'd had to leave our dogs at home. Without a warm Poodle body to caress, her hands must have felt empty.

"Surely you're not worried about the symposium?" I asked.

"Heavens, no. I could lead a judging seminar in my sleep. It's Victor Durbin who's a concern. Along with that dratted Empire Poodle Club specialty that will be running at the same time. All things considered, it's drawn quite an entry."

All things considered, indeed.

Victor Durbin was a Miniature Poodle breeder and a former member of Connecticut's Paugussett Club. He'd been asked to resign from the club several years earlier after the board discovered that Victor had been allowing Cocker Spaniel and Schnauzer owners to breed their bitches to his Mini Poodle stud dogs. The resulting mixed-breed litters of Cockapoos and Schnoodles were flooding the local pet shops.

After his expulsion from the club, Victor claimed to have changed his ways. He'd petitioned to be reinstated. His request was summarily denied. Aunt Peg had led that charge—but a majority of the other members agreed with her. Most hoped that Victor would quietly move on. Perhaps find another breed with which to become involved.

But Victor had had other ideas. Instead, he'd decided to form his own Poodle club. Though the tri-state area was already home to several other affiliate clubs, Victor

was undeterred. He'd taken the other groups' member-
ship rosters, and proceeded to search their ranks for disgruntled members who could be convinced to jump ship
and join his nascent club. Once he had enough names,
Victor had doggedly shepherded his Empire Poodle Club
through the steps required for AKC accreditation.

EPC had received a license to hold its inaugural Poodle specialty the previous year. A date that fell on the day
before Westminster had been applied for and approved. A
Manhattan venue was booked. The single-breed show
would take place in the ballroom of a hotel on Seventh
Avenue. It happened to be the same hotel where the Paugussett Poodle Club was hosting its judging seminar at
the same time.

Nobody thought that was a coincidence. Least of all
Aunt Peg.

"You don't need to worry about Victor." Sam exited
onto the Henry Hudson Parkway to head south. "His specialty show is in the second floor ballroom. The conference room for the symposium is on the fourth floor.
There's no reason that your paths should even cross."

"Our paths have already crossed, in a manner of
speaking," Aunt Peg replied tartly. I couldn't blame her
for being annoyed. "It's perfectly obvious that more people would have signed up for the seminar if there weren't
a competing Poodle event happening right downstairs."

"If more people had signed up, the club would have
had to book a bigger room," I pointed out. Poodles' three
varieties—Toy, Miniature, and Standard—meant the breed
offered aspiring judges entrée into both the Toy and Non-
Sporting Groups. That automatically made them a popular breed for which to apply. "Even with the specialty,

there are more than a hundred people coming to learn more about Poodles from you."

"You needn't sound so surprised," Aunt Peg said drily.

Sam cast her a glance. "Actually I'm a little surprised that the Westminster show committee is allowing you to participate in both this symposium and their event tomorrow. We all know that they frown on even a hint of bias or favoritism. The group and Best in Show judges are barred from attending the show before they arrive to do their part, for that very reason."

"The committee would indeed be very unhappy if I was socializing with exhibitors who might later find themselves in my ring," Aunt Peg admitted. "But in this case, they agreed that I could hardly get up to much trouble in the company of my fellow judges."

"They must not know you nearly as well as we do," I said under my breath.

"I'm sorry." Aunt Peg turned in her seat again. "Did you say something?"

Fortunately, I was saved from having to answer by the buzzing of my phone. Our home number came up on the screen. Knowing that between the symposium and the dog show we'd be busy all day, Sam and I had left our kids at home in Connecticut.

Davey was fourteen, and halfway through his first year of high school. He was babysitting his younger brother, Kevin, who would turn five next month. Both boys shared our interest in Standard Poodles. But Kevin was too young to follow us around quietly for hours at a time. And Davey had no desire to devote a weekend day listening to Aunt Peg deliver a lecture. That sounded entirely too much like schoolwork to him.

I lifted the phone to my ear. "Hey, Davey, what's up? Is everything okay?"

"Yup." Now that he's a teenager, Davey doesn't expend extra words on his parents. "But we need carrots."

"Carrots?" My sons were asking for vegetables? That was a first.

"Kev and I are building a snowman in the backyard. The dogs are helping. Except Bud. You know."

I did. Bud, a small spotted mutt we'd adopted two summers earlier, was more trouble than our five Standard Poodles combined. I gave Davey props for the snowman idea, though. We'd had four inches of fresh, powdery snow on Friday night. Now on Sunday morning, it would be packed just right for building.

"You want a carrot for the nose?" I asked.

Davey laughed. "You would think—but no. Kevin wants them for his ears. So they stick straight up like Bud's."

Technically only one of Bud's ears stuck up. The other flopped forward over his eye. It wasn't worth debating.

"Did you check the vegetable bin in the bottom of the refrigerator?"

"I looked there first. The only thing in there is onions."

"Ewww!" I heard Kevin say in the background.

"Yes, I can see how that wouldn't work." I looked up at Sam. "Are we out of carrots?"

He shrugged. Traffic was light on a Sunday morning. Even so he was paying attention to the route as he pulled off the highway onto a side street.

"What do we have that's long and skinny?" I mused, putting the phone on speaker.

"How about straws?" Aunt Peg offered from the front seat.

"Too small," Davey replied. "This is a big snowman. Almost a snow monster."

"It's a snow monster." Kevin giggled. "Except he needs ears."

"Wait a minute," I said. "How about a couple of hot dogs? That could work. They'd even wiggle in the wind like real ears."

"Good idea," Davey agreed. "I'm on it." He ended the connection.

"Hmmph," said Aunt Peg.

I tucked the phone back in my pocket. "Now what?"

"Am I to understand that your kitchen is lacking in vegetables but well stocked with hot dogs?"

I wanted to deny it, but really there was no point.

"Something like that," I said.

"Sometimes you feed kids what they'll eat rather than what's good for them," Sam mentioned.

*Thanks, honey.*

Aunt Peg wasn't appeased. "It sounds as though I feed my Poodles better food than you give your children," she huffed.

"You might," I agreed easily. I would never argue with Aunt Peg about canine care. Hers or anyone else's.

"Stop squabbling, you two." Sam turned on his blinker and turned into the entrance to a parking garage. "We've arrived."

# Chapter
# Two

We entered the Manhattan hotel lobby loaded down with gear.

Sam was carrying the grooming table tucked beneath his arm. Aunt Peg had a briefcase filled with slides and notes she'd brought from home. I was holding a box that contained handouts for the attendees. The only thing we didn't have with us was a live Poodle.

The audience for the seminar would be made up of people who wanted to learn how to judge Poodles. With that in mind, Aunt Peg wanted to display a dog that looked exactly as it would appear before them in the show ring. Coral, the teenage Standard Poodle that she and Davey had been showing together, was too young to serve as a model. However Crawford Langley—a professional handler who was showing at the Empire specialty on the second floor—had offered to supply her with a demo dog later that afternoon.

I looked at my watch as we headed for the elevators. It was eleven a.m. Both the specialty and the seminar were scheduled to begin at noon. Once again, probably not a coincidence.

"After I deliver this stuff to the conference room, I'm going down to spend some time at the show," I told Aunt Peg. Though the judging wouldn't start for another hour, the ballroom would already be full. Poodle exhibitors always arrived early since they had plenty of pre-ring grooming to do.

Aunt Peg turned to me in mock outrage. "You're not going to attend my seminar?"

We'd been over this before. Possibly a dozen times. I'd lost count of how often this complaint had come up during the past month.

"Not all of it," I said. "First, I'm going to the specialty."

"You're passing up a wonderful learning opportunity."

"How do you figure that?" I asked. "You've been lecturing me for years. It hardly seems possible you might have more stuff to say that I haven't heard yet."

Aunt Peg looked at me down her nose. "I don't see why. I learn new things all the time."

I juggled the heavy box to one side and pushed the button for the elevator. "Then it's a good thing Sam will be listening to your entire talk. He'll be able to fill me in on anything I miss."

The elevator door slid open. We fit ourselves inside. "Thank goodness one of my relatives is here to support me," Aunt Peg sniffed.

"Yes," I said, punching the next button with more force than was strictly necessary. "Lucky you."

Sam was standing behind Aunt Peg, trying not to grin. He'd always been her favorite. I was used to that by now.

"I should think you'd want a first-hand report on Victor Durbin's specialty," I mentioned. "It's the Empire Club's first attempt to stage an event—and in New York City, no less. I wonder if they've taken into account all the things that could possibly go wrong?"

Aunt Peg considered that, then nodded. "You have a point. I suppose you'll be making yourself useful, after all."

It was a small victory, but I'd take it. Especially as it meant I could now attend the specialty with a clear conscience.

The conference room was open and waiting for us. Rows of folding chairs had already been set in place. There was a slide projector in the back of the room. A dais in the front held an empty table and a podium with a microphone. Behind it, a white screen had been pulled down from the ceiling.

I put the box I'd been carrying down on the table. A hotel employee came over to make sure that Aunt Peg had everything she needed. Several Paugussett Club members had also been waiting for her arrival. They gathered around too.

Aunt Peg appeared to be in good hands. That was all I needed to know. I sketched Sam a wave and made a hasty exit before my esteemed relative could change her mind.

The Poodle show awaited downstairs. *Excellent.*

The conference room had been quiet and nearly empty. By contrast, the ballroom on the second floor hummed with activity.

Dog shows generate their own particular buzz of excitement. Some exhibitors thrive on the winning, and the thrill of competition. Others come to show off the best dogs that their breeding programs have produced. Many treat the shows as social events, since they're a wonderful opportunity to spend a day surrounded by friends.

Indeed, the first dog shows were simply gatherings of neighbors who brought their dogs together for the purpose of debating their relative merits. Though the sport has grown tremendously since then, at its core, not a lot has changed.

Breeders still strive to produce the finest dogs they can, always bearing in mind the purpose for which the breed was intended. And judges and exhibitors still argue over which dog is actually the best. It all makes for a lively exchange. As well as the occasional impassioned dispute.

A specialty is a dog show devoted to a single breed of dog. On this weekend before Westminster, a dozen different breed clubs were holding specialties in Manhattan. With the top dogs coming to New York for the big show, it made sense for the clubs to capitalize on the influx of out-of-town exhibitors. In various ballrooms around the city, spectators could enjoy watching Boston Terriers, Pekingese, and French Bulldogs all strut their stuff.

The ballroom I entered, however, held only Poodles. Just what I wanted to see.

A large rectangular ring had been set up in the center of the room. Though it was currently empty, the perimeter of the floor had already been lined with nonslip mats. The judge's table was in place. All was ready for business.

The day's exhibitors had arranged their setups around

the outside of the ring. Crates were stacked. Tack boxes were open. Blow dryers were in use. Dozens of Poodles were already out on their tabletops, being groomed. Thanks to the layout of the room, exhibitors would be able to prepare their dogs and spectate at the same time.

According to the judging schedule, Standard Poodles would be shown first. They were followed by the Miniatures, then Toys. As the largest variety, Standards took the longest to prepare for the ring. It was no surprise, then, that most tables held the bigger dogs, while the Minis and Toys waited their turn in nearby crates.

I paused just inside the doorway to the room. It only took me a few seconds to locate my good friends Crawford Langley and his life partner and handling assistant, Terry Denunzio. When I spotted their setup, my eyebrows rose. Even in the crowded ballroom, Terry was hard to miss.

Which was probably the point, I thought, smothering a laugh.

Terry has a flamboyant streak a mile wide. Since the last time I'd seen him, he had changed his hair color again. Blond before, he'd now opted for a shade not often found in nature.

Perhaps he'd been inspired by the Westminster's own club colors, I realized. Either that or an eggplant. Standing out amidst the beautifully coiffed Poodles with their black, brown, and white coats, Terry's hair was a brilliant shade of purple. I wondered what Crawford thought of that.

Probably not much.

Terry and Crawford were opposites in many ways. Maybe that was why they made such a great couple. In his sixties, Crawford was staid and dignified. The con-

"That figures." I sighed. "This place is crammed with Poodles. His specialty drew a terrific entry. Victor must be feeling very pleased with himself."

"Points are points, Melanie," Crawford interjected. "And Victor hired a fine Poodle judge in Louise Bixby. Some of us have to take our opportunities where we find them."

Strictly speaking, I knew that wasn't true. For a handler like Crawford there would always be judges who enjoyed seeing him in their show ring, and who were more than happy to reward the dogs he brought them. Crawford never lacked for opportunities to win.

To be fair, however, I could also understand the appeal of wanting to nab a nice win now, right before Westminster. All the top competitors were in town. For this one week, the attention of the entire dog community would be focused on New York City.

A success here would be a big feather in any handler's cap. Not only that, but a specialty win today would give a dog added impetus to do well in the breed judging at Westminster tomorrow.

"I'd like to see a topknot in that Standard," Crawford mentioned pointedly.

Terry had just finished brushing the Standard bitch. He sat her up on the table. Reaching into the tack box, he grabbed a knitting needle for making parts and a bag of tiny, colored rubber bands.

"It's coming right now," he said.

"Maybe if your fingers were moving as fast as your mouth, it would already be in place," Crawford replied.

I was pretty sure that was my cue to move along. Considering how prickly Crawford had been lately, I had no

summate professional, he'd been at the top of the handling game for more years than I'd been going to dog shows. Terry was closer to my age; we were both edging toward forty. He was a blithe, free spirit who took almost nothing seriously. Except his longstanding relationship with Crawford.

I made my way quickly through the setups that clogged the area between us. Some of the exhibitors I passed were familiar to me, as we were frequent competitors at the local shows. Others had come from all over the country; they were in town now for the Westminster show. Previously I'd only seen their Poodles on the pages of the glossy canine publications. I couldn't wait to have a chance to admire them in person.

"Air kiss," Terry said as I approached. There was a white Standard Poodle lying down on the grooming table between us. He leaned over it and aimed a pair of smooches in my general direction.

I followed suit. It wouldn't do to muss his make-up. Then I walked around the table, lifted a hand, and feathered it through his locks. "Really?" I said.

He batted his eyes. "Don't you love it?"

"I don't know." I tipped my head to one side and considered the look. "I'm still deciding. What does Crawford think?"

The older handler was standing no more than four feet away. He must have heard my question. Even so, he didn't turn around. I sighed and looked at Terry. He frowned, then gave a slight shrug.

Apparently I still hadn't been forgiven.

The previous summer I'd done something that betrayed Crawford's trust. I knew he was a very private person—and that he wouldn't appreciate my delving into his past. Sam had warned me not to do it. But at the time the risk had seemed worth taking.

I'd learned what I needed to know, and Terry had been enormously grateful for the way things had turned out. But despite his efforts to bring about a reconciliation, my relationship with Crawford had been strained ever since.

"Good morning, Melanie," the handler said now. He still didn't turn around. "Standards go in the ring in less than an hour. We're a little busy here."

*Well.* I guessed that meant I wouldn't be sticking around to chat.

"It's okay," Terry said quickly. He reached out and laid a hand on my arm so I wouldn't move away. "I'm a man of many talents. I can talk and brush at the same time."

Crawford harrumphed under his breath. I winced. Terry ignored him.

"So," he said brightly. "Where's McDreamy today?"

He was referring to Sam, of course. Apparently I wasn't the only one who had a crush on my husband. And no wonder. Sam had slate blue eyes, a killer smile, and charm to spare. Not to mention that body.

"You know Sam hates it when you call him that," I said.

"Yes, I know. Ask me if I care." Terry stuck out his tongue. "If he was here, I wouldn't do it. Hence the question."

"He's upstairs with Aunt Peg. You know, at PPC's judging seminar?"

Terry picked up his pin brush and went back to work while we talked. The white Standard on the table had her eyes closed. She was probably asleep.

"Of course I know about the seminar. Who doesn't? Margaret Turnbull offering a master class in evaluating a

Poodle for the show ring? This weekend, that's probably the hottest ticket in town."

"Don't let Aunt Peg hear you say that." I laughed. "Her ego is big enough as it is."

"And justifiably so," Crawford muttered. Still facing the other way, he'd declined to join our conversation. But he was obviously paying attention.

"Anyway, I don't know about a hot ticket," I said. "The seminar is full, but it would have drawn a bigger crowd if Victor Durbin hadn't scheduled this show to take place opposite it."

Terry looked surprised. "You think he did that on purpose?"

"Don't you?"

Terry considered the question. "I knew there was bad blood between them. Peg was on the board when he was kicked out of the Paugussett Club, wasn't she?"

I nodded.

"But that happened years ago. Is he still holding a grudge?" Terry looked around for a misting bottle.

I plucked one off a nearby table and handed it to him. "You tell me. The date for Aunt Peg's seminar was announced more than a year ago. The Empire Club could have scheduled their specialty to take place yesterday. But they didn't. Victor's the one who created the conflict. It seems to me like he wanted to draw a line on the ground between them, then make people choose sides."

I paused to gaze around the room. "Speaking of Victor, I haven't seen him yet. I assume he must be here somewhere?"

"Oh, he's here all right." Terry smirked. "Last time I saw him, he was strutting around the ballroom like a rooster who thought he owned the barnyard."

intention of over staying my welcome. At least not any more than I already had.

"I'll see you guys later," I said. "Good luck! Louise Bixby should love your Mini special. Topper's been on a roll."

Topper was Champion Gold Dust High Top, a sparkling apricot Miniature Poodle with whom Crawford had been tearing up the show ring for the previous three months. A finished champion—also known as a specials dog—he was entered both here and on Monday at Westminster. I knew Crawford and Terry were really hoping that the Mini would win the variety there and go on to compete in the Non-Sporting Group.

"Shush!" said Terry. "Don't jinx us." He glanced at his partner to see if he'd heard me.

I hadn't expected that. "Since when did Crawford become superstitious?"

Terry rolled his eyes as if he was surprised I even had to ask. And maybe he had a point.

"It's Westminster week," he said. "Everyone wants a win here more than anything. That means we're all on edge."

# Connect with Us

Visit us online at
**KensingtonBooks.com**
to read more from your favorite authors, see books
by series, view reading group guides, and more.

**Join us on social media**

for sneak peeks, chances to win books and prize packs,
and to share your thoughts with other readers.

facebook.com/kensingtonpublishing
twitter.com/kensingtonbooks

## Tell us what you think!

To share your thoughts, submit a review,
or sign up for our eNewsletters, please visit:
**KensingtonBooks.com/TellUs.**